"Gary Lutz is one of my very favorite prose stylists."

—Dennis Cooper

"One would call these lives adrift except that would suggest they once were safely moored and docked. In Lutz's world there is only ever the open sea of failed (non)relationships, with no land in sight, the characters' only rudder being the extreme care taken in the words they choose to express their own misery. In each of these stories, the lonely anonymity of a narrator's misfit existence vies with the glorious singularity of his or her discourse to offer a marvelous, raw tension. *Partial List of People to Bleach* is at once cruelly honest, precisely painful, and beautifully rendered."

—Brian Evenson

"Ominous, creepy, and mind-bendingly alert, Lutz lays out each of his perfectly crafted sentences with the sinister exactitude and obsessive care of Beckett's Molloy shuffling stones between his pockets. These musically torqued, masterful sentences, bedecked with elegant syntax and the glint of a razor-sharp locution, accrue into an equally surprising and angular narrative, creating an explosively original combination—stories as muddy and dark in their exploration of domesticity as they are crystalline and celebratory in their structure and language."

—*Rain Taxi Review of Books*

Also by Gary Lutz:
Stories in the Worst Way
I Looked Alive
Divorcer

PARTIAL LIST OF PEOPLE TO BLEACH

GARY LUTZ

Future Tense Books
portland, oregon

Partial List of People to Bleach
Fictions and an Essay by Gary Lutz

© 2013 by Gary Lutz
All rights reserved. Printed in the United States of America.
Book design and cover design by Bryan Coffelt.
Set in Adobe Caslon Pro.

ISBN 978-1-892061-44-7

Future Tense Books
PO Box 42416
Portland, OR 97242
www.futuretensebooks.com

for Thomas Vasko

CONTENTS

FOREWORD

Huffe-snuffe, okay? Right, right, have not the slightest
notion what huffe-snuffe means. Know only that, as far as
I am concerned, it looks great, has one of those ferociously
endangered hyphens in the middle of it, and that it, huffe-
snuffe, came up this morning in the course of my reading
here and there in Hugh Kenner's *A Homemade World*, which
book, to my mind, is a pretty swell book, you got me? Look,
I'm not saying this has anything to do with Gary Lutz or
with his *Partial List* and so on, or with, unless it's supposed
to be nor with, the publisher of same. Fine, fine, I guess good
manners, had that etiquette had the least little control of me,
would have called for the distinguishing of this element from
that element with quotation marks or some such typological
(typographical?) device, setting this apart from that, as per,
for instance, nor with—thus: "nor with" or *nor with*. Are
you following me? I am going to take it for granted you are
following me, but even if you aren't, what am I to do about
it? Simplify matters? Go about my business here, in Lutz's
behalf, not to mention in probably yours, in a less congested
way? Sorry, no can do. Well, I can, I expect I can—but
won't. Fair enough? You bet it's fair enough. I mean, face it,
let's face it—I was reading Kenner, on the one hand, and
struggling to set up a new TV, on the other, when the day's
post came and therein the appeal from Lutz's benefactor to
speak up, introduction-wise, for Lutz. Swell. Am I happy
to do that? Yes, I am happy to do that! Also proud, pleased,

tickled to death, to affiliate myself with you-know-who and with the reprint of you-know-whose *Partial List* and so forth and so on. Except, pay attention—there's the Kenner disquisition for me to get back to and, not unchallengingly, working out the facilitating, wire-wise, of this new TV of mine—a, hey, Insignia. Sure, sure, would have laid out for the Samsung if I had any brains, but figured better to save the bucks and throw in with the Best Buy house-brand, which I did, which I did, but which hook-up—I mean, getting it (the TV) going—I've gone ahead and put on hold for a trice (ditto Kenner, ditto the Kenner) while I handle this Lutz thing—not anywhere close to lustrously maybe (I'm distracted, I'm too distracted for luster)—but, you know, officially adequately. Uh-oh, is it not unlikely you've been sitting there and forgotten all about huffe-snuffe? I did. Well, almost—I almost did. You think I should hasten myself to the dictionary apropos of this (huffe-snuffe) or, mal-apropos of it, skip it and just keep it (huffe-snuffe) a mystery?

Well, to me, anyway.

Anyhow, that's, um, it.

Trice over, trice finished, which word I do not, even remotely, know the definition of, either. My golly, all this is starting to seem to me, Lutz-wise, uncannily appropriate. Perhaps even indicative, mayhaps a jot luminescent. If so, if you get something from this you could not have gotten by reason of a reasonable approach, you're just where it's best for you to be—at the beginning of a one-of-a-kind experience, at the beginning of the impudently singular, at the beginning of—oh, to heck with it!—beginningness.

— Gordon Lish, New York, June, 2013

HOME, SCHOOL, OFFICE

I remember buying something once—I can't remember what—in the stationery aisle of an all-night drugstore, something I did not need. All I remember is what the card accompanying it said: "101 Uses for Home, School, Office." I remember thinking there was a home, a school, an office in my life, so why not? Make the purchase, look alive. This was how long ago?

HOME

The home in this case was actually two homes. First, my apartment, which was just mounds of filthied clothes, newspapers, index cards, depilatories, razors, and paper plates forming a ragged little semicircle around wherever I happened to be crouched on the floor when I was home. (I owned no furniture; I was afraid of heights.) And then her place, a house she rented, a place she vacuumed and dusted, where I slept with her, where she made the bed. She had a name, a job, a kid, a parrot, a couple of ex-husbands, relatives, neighbors she concerned. When she wasn't drunk, I was her project.

SCHOOL

I taught at a school, a college—actually, a community college. The students hated me, and most who got stuck in my courses eventually dropped. I would step into a classroom on the first day of the term, and a good third of the kids, furious that I was going to be the teacher, would get up and walk out. On those who remained, I got my revenge by ladling out all A's—even an A for the kid who slept through my entire last term, because I was jealous of his frictionless, rubber-limbed sleep. I would often want to stop talking—there was never any discussion; I filled the room with words for seventy-five-minute sessions, displacing the air with sequences of salival syllables arranged to give one the feeling, afterward, of having heard something like a lecture, something that could survive on a margin-doodled notebook page in a plausible outline of a plausible topic—so that I would not wake the kid up, even though it was obvious he could sleep through disquiets of any kind. (My own sleep was and continues to be a tiresome business—battering, sloppy, unproductive.) Shall I admit that more than once I wanted to share that kid's sleep—i.e., to be fucked and fucked and fucked by him until I bled?

OFFICE

I shared what had once been a large supply closet with a history teacher, a woman who smelled like the exhaust fumes of a bus and who canceled her classes at least once a week. One morning, as I was repositioning books and papers on my desk, an elaborately coiled pubic hair—it called to mind a notebook spiral—slid out of a folder labeled "TO BE FILED" that I had been trying to find a new place for, and landed on the carpet. This was carpet the color of pavement. My officemate was nowhere to be found, and the office door was shut, and locked, so I got down on my knees and sought out the hair. I thought the thing would be a cinch to find, but it wasn't. I just couldn't put my finger on anything. I borrowed a piece of cellophane tape from my officemate's desk (I had never asked for any supplies, but my officemate had a metal tape dispenser—a big thing, a console, really—and a stapler and a hole-puncher and a telephone) and thought that if I dragged the strip of tape, with the adhesive side down, along every square inch of the carpet, the hair would eventually

cling to the tape. But after about five minutes, I gave up—
not because the phone rang (it was my officemate's phone,
obviously, and it never rang) or because there was a knock
at the door (I had signed up for five office hours a week,
but nobody ever came by except for students asking after
my officemate or dropping off get-well-soon balloons), but
because I did not know up to what point, to what extent, I
was supposed to keep going along with my life.

KANSAS CITY, MISSOULA

I moved in with my sister and her girlfriend after my little marriage had started to wear itself to the bone again.

I was twenty-seven, mostly unknown to myself, known best by my sister, who said, "You won't have to do anything yet."

But I had always made sad work of persons. Even now, in these later, these punchier times, everything is just modicums of what it once was.

My sister and her girlfriend were, both of them, paralegals. They were renting a house at the confusing end of town. This was out beyond where people still felt any need to mix.

The girlfriend was the tallest of us three. She had lots of that mobile jewelry all over her. Her body seemed to crowd around her life in ways that kept her from being too social with me.

But my sister was the sackier one. There were blurts of blue in her hair.

My first full day was a workday for them. They had me using the edges of one of those disposable-razor caps to scrape away the crud from the insides of their tub. They would be wanting a bath, a long, lemon-laden, embubbled soak, they had said, after they came home and before they took on the night's carnal charges.

They would be arriving antsily together in that nonnative sedan of theirs.

I had to shove a brood of soaps aside.

The tub's guck came off in a powderish gray. This took hours, but what was time to someone with nothing to wait for but take-out pad thai, hoi polloi, potpie, whatever they were calling it?

The house was actually more of a cottage, with bookcases built bluntly into the walls. The books I could not exactly read (I had disorders), but I could land a hand onto a page, spread my fingers, then make out whichever words that showed in between, though these were mostly just ingredients of words:

firt leen bini
aze   oli

They shut their bedroom door at night.

Mornings, I went through their drawers—but things were much too plush and tingly for me in there, all that underwear inalienably theirs, plus some shapely drugs, mostly robin's-egg-blue and dazing.

I took another of the tabs. It was quick to get me feeling renewedly mortalized and minute.

I couldn't log on to either of their boxy old laptops. No diaries or journals or such for me to see whatever each might have finally dared rue about the other. Those two more likely lacked even a line of wiseacre poetry to their name.

I could have written a poem for or against them right then and there, and tried to, something merrimental and penciled, but it got to be all about my own catchy life and what all had gotten caught in it—the set bedtimes and slant-tip tweezers, any old TV screen with the power off, the less-than-a-year-left stuff that dragged on and on, the chances begged for, the overnight bags that were actually technically for the next day, if you woke up and the world was still looking coy.

I needed to find something better to know like the back of my hand.

The last time I had gone looking, I'd found that woman with the tiny floes of green in her eyes. This was a woman like nothing else floral at all. She had had concussions, and blackouts, and was still blinky years later when she turned up looking ousted from everything peaceable in the species. So, yeah, I loved her calamitously and however little. But she was a braggart, a cheat, and a back-stabber. I'll keep her mostly out of this reminiscent business, though. I'm under orders to tend to just about any other hill of beans.

Regardless, I'll venture that marriage spreads itself filmily and spherically around two people until you're doing your best to poke your way back out.

Truth be told, I felt less joined than merely jointed to her in little fiscal fashions.

She would say, "Are we ever even talking about the same thing?"

She hoped to be a guitarist. It would have had to be one of those half-size guitars. The songs were going to be bouncy and sagacious about having a cunt with more mystique than most. For a minute there, in the stairwell, her singing voice got something trapped in it, a real shiver that brought you revealments from afar.

Making her way up the steps was a girl who must have heard. The girl looked to be about that age when instead of places to go there were only worlds to come.

They just shook hands at first, exchanged names hard-headedly, then sniveled until the two of them were kissing.

I didn't hear from my wife for a while.

I'm not telling you anything I won't have already one day come to have known about myself, at least the parts about life's not being right for everyone, and how I've no reason to know why; but for a couple of semesters, I'd pushed myself over at the community college, the one they had set up in the older hangars. My fingers kept driving themselves into the books until every binding gave up the ghost. One of the profs, some even-minded soul, took me aside, said, "All work and no play." I said, "I'll play when I'm dead." But it was a stretch, and then I took up with that man who day in and day out looked loveproof and bloated.

What—all that water and blood in him wasn't enough to drown his sorrows either?

His story was that I was using him just to brush up against myself. But I must have looked redundant even off on my own.

Men, you must know, are behind everything, meaning only laggard, backward, passé.

But I keep coming back to my wife as if she weren't the one coming back to me standing pat.

This was all in that make-do conurbation between the state's two hardening and unfavored cities nobody even snooped around in anymore.

We didn't really tell anybody about the marriage. Whom could we have told?

Her sister was dead, and her parents weren't the type you would ever once think to describe, and as for friends, there were none left aside from me, though she might have sent notes, potshot postcards, to lorn pharmacists she had leaned on, or mentors long spurned, or pushover crisis-hot-line troubleshooters, or any other sobber who might have once bashfully asked her to piss on him as a finale to something long since finished anyway.

As for my acquaintances, I knew a man who kept daintily to himself in an enlarged house with six sinks and a tub from which the water, he claimed, would never completely run away. It had the plumbers stumped. He was hit with bills you wouldn't believe. He was thorough-hearted and easily wowed. I called him every now and then to go over the eventualities.

"It's all been pushed back," he would say, then hang up, then not answer when I kept redialing, thinking: by which he had meant what—it's been moved forward or further behind?

I had a dictionary, but it was the kind that hedged on everything.

"Bound, adj.," or so it said, meant just the opposite of "bound, vb."

So I tried to keep my wife to the fore and laid off sex.

We lived in the perfect timing of our passions for other people.

Some people, I now see, are idea people. The idea might be only: Eschew bloodbaths.

My mother had never done much besides lose her heart to the dial tone. It must have seemed a threnody of a kind. That was in the times of landlines only. I believe she lived mostly in silhouette.

It was my father who had taught me it would be disloyal to buy another town's newspaper, even the one from the town just down the road, where the people liked it when the hours finally got themselves all balled up into a day that could just roll itself right off from them.

So my sister's girlfriend, to let something be known: I did in fact try her out in their bed. It's no debauch, though, if the other party is mutinous in even the twiddliest way against your own sis. She buttoned her lip. Everything went without brunt. Next morn, she said, "You're a man still here. You're a breach of peace."

But I've never been very immediate in things. I've skipped out on myself every time.

My wife had married me in a huff. There had been somebody else, somebody before me and later to come back—a man of clean riches. Any affection from me went right through her.

I'll say one thing for her, though:

She looked for all the world.

YEARS OF AGE

My sisters had turned out to be women who wore their hair speculatively, lavishing it forward into swells, or loading it again with clips, barrettes. The younger worked for a store that still had a notions department, a dry-goods department, a toilet with a coin slot on the door. Her affections raced in undaring ovals around co-workers.

The other lived on her own in a safehold of foldaways and one-player card games with crueler and crueler rules. She had a couple of dogs that she wanted to see something of the world.

I was the middle child, but never the central one. I had gone through life as the unencircled son, unfetched.

The three of us were heeders and continuers, yes, but mostly resemblers bent on coarsening the resemblance.

•

I had been a suggestible kid, senseless in all I foresaw. I'd had that pair of shiftful sisters, and parents: the kind who taught you to tell time, then taught you that time would tell. High school I had liked—the hourly hallway travel, the breezy hygiene of the girls—and in college most of the profs shook your hand on your happy way out of the amphitheatre. One subject would eclipse another until there was a totter to my grades.

A diploma was at length made out to me, and I was free to apply for openings. I liked the festive attention allowed me at interviews—the questions put to me pointedly but

PARTIAL LIST OF PEOPLE TO BLEACH   21

unpersonally. My first job involved scourging printouts with proofreaders' marks in a metropolis of sorts mocked up for regional commerce beside a thin, palling river. I prinked about the offices in baleful well-being, maybe awaiting ovations.

Or was I already taking the long view—that the world we lived in stood in the way of another world, one where you need not keep going back into things with your eyes wide open?

I took to taking things calmly and degenerately.

•

I moved to the forefront of the city, shared an apartment divided four scarcely distinct ways, now and then brought home discouraged hitchhikers or delicately shaven teenagers—wrathful, faceless kids easily regaled with things neither strange nor true. I thus got roughed up in my roommates' regard, found "FOR SALE" signs taped everywhere on my car. Then the first, brute months of a new year. I spaced things out in my luggage and hauled it all to the outskirts. I became one of those secretive types who want you to know everything about them except what should most catch the eye.

People, in truth, had got the *wrong* wrong ideas about me—that I responded well to cosmetics; that I had already come to know most of the disrobers in our town of halfway houses and rehab socials; that my teeth had been sewn tight into my gums with thick black thread.

In awful point of fact, I rewrote my rent checks until the dollar-amount and signatural hurrah was just so, and I called my parents almost any Sunday. I would force myself to talk for exactly twelve minutes, the better to counter criticisms that I could never be kept on the line for more than ten.

I would have to answer the same question every time: "Why are you always so out of breath like that?"

•

Shall I say that I eventually shamed myself away from men, though they had been just boys, actually—boys too much alike in the rough patter of their pulse? They were happily acrid in shorts almost too long to be shorts.

It's not every day I let any of them come cohering back. But there was one whom I will call by some other name, *Floke*, and who called me both timid and vicious—tender in only an investigative way.

•

Or, rather, there were men I offered the luxury of witnessed private conduct, and women who set out bridge mix or pretzel twists, women with colorless good looks, women who picked fights with their bodies.

I always walked away a differently unchosen person.

My life neither wended nor entailed.

•

The one at whose side I worked that summer was deep-set in family heartaches, and facially inhumane, but she sometimes came out from behind all the etiquette.

Eleven was the only clock word she liked. She would insist it sounded lilting and relenting to her.

For me, though, the hour itself—the work-shift one, I mean, and not its trimmer twin in late evening—did not slope toward anything better. I never budged for lunch, and I liked to do myself in a little. I would postpone a piss until I had to brave rapids, practically. (There was a vessel I kept beneath my desk.)

This was the property-management division. We were sectored off from the rest of headquarters by little more than particleboard. The job required the luxurious useless indoor fortitude it has always been my fortune to enjoy.

•

Then some unsought weeks with a silkened fright of a girl with unfellowly elbows, lively fatalities in her thinking. She had a ring of relations around her—impressionable cousinry, commanding aunts with bracelets by the silverous slew—and we moved in with her parents, early retirees, who swanked away at the prospect of the two of us unpairing before the year got thinned of its holidays. Her father would stand outside our room, knock gallantly on the door, say, "We hear you in there." Then the mother would say, "We most certainly do not." It was her reproofs that counted.

•

Men of my kind kept cramming themselves into marriages, violated hindquarters and all. I mugged for a minister late one morning myself.

This was hazing July, and the day just burned away.

My wife came from a family with vaulted closets, kitchens with doors that locked. Every dress the woman wore had to have vents, slits, pinholes. She drank excitative mixed drinks of her own fixing, was swayable in her credos, drove home the sobering groceries.

Her hair had something almost auroral about it, plenty of sparkle in its upper reaches. But she wasn't eating.

•

When the day came that she wanted something frothed and resolving to daub onto her face, I walked her to a makeup counter at H--- Brothers. A saleslady came over. We made it sound as if we were picking out a gift.

Was the skin about which we were barely making a peep a dry skin, or an oily one, or was it splotched, or papery, or combination? What was the one thing the woman—if the intended recipient was, indeed, a woman—wanted most to change?

"Should we be telling people?"

•

I might have kept going through life repeating: Consider the source!

•

There was, a while afterward, just one other taker, somebody else at city hall, a man who leaned on me during the last-ditch derisions of election year. (A stuffy, unbowing couch in his office, a provisioning little fridge, curtains and blinds both.) He expected to compound some things he still felt for his wife with his unriotous feelings for me, then come up with a new, totaling emotion that he could offer to the woman he wanted to clean his life out with. She was a recent hire in the prothonotary's office, level-voiced and unshifting. Mistily immediate one minute, undivinable the next.

As for the man, there was little he still did in his role as my resister. I started bringing things home from the library—magazines mostly, the pages brightly outdated. Touching whatever someone else had touched first was going to be fellowship enough for me.

This was punctual, unbrilliant winter. My car got harder to start. The thing just scoffed, razzed. The library stayed open later and later. The one I liked behind the circulation desk had lips dulled plumly, some final drifts of girlhood at peril in her voice. A becoming boniness to the fingers, and that hardening and seaming of the face achieved, I was certain, from having seen too soon the pleading in things.

I must have been hoping for someone deep-eyed and hampered and unfancied like that, someone with consolingly different dislikes—pretty-witted antipathies I would not want to trump.

This library had a back-corner department of cassettes thick-cased into sets, series. I signed some out, drew myself into a few. I did not own a player, but I would poke the cap of a pen through one of the hubs in a cassette, jostle the tape forward a little that way. Such were my heaves, my advances, in the hours before I would pass myself back into the unmonopolizing sleep of my nerveless, earliest thirties.

•

Hard to imagine anyone's ever having had cause enough to wonder what in my life might have once been worth a count—dying adorations, maybe, or playsome enamorations going way back to nursery school, or any hands most recently mislaid on me, then on bedposts, then on banisters on the bullying way back down the stairs.

•

My sisters were just sturdier, vulval versions of myself. We kept in touch by tardy and typoed e-mail. Greeting cards arrived on time to clear things up again about Mom. ("Hi there guys. Sorry for the form note.")

When I asked how things were going, the answers came out more like pledges than anecdotes.

The older of them rode the bus over one night and knocked, tunicked and flip-flopping, a bismuth-pink on her lips. She had gotten herself a flu shot some days before, and would I have a go at the Band-Aid? She whisked up her sleeve. Her bare upper arm was pale and asquish.

I saw her home afterward to her troves.

My younger sister threw herself into her work, battled away at largely moony evenings. For a time, our feelings ran parallel toward the same woman. A yearning for her firmed in us both.

This woman put wrong names to our faces, and there were oddened tilts and tonings to her voice as often as we approached. Her wardrobe was a rowdydow of oranges, beckoning reds.

Eyes an acorn color.

Hair she kept ruckussed upward.

A finger sometimes presuming upon a front tooth—to test the sureness of its set, its hold?

These were weeks of endangering heat. My sister and I were of like violences of mind about this unrelished, unensnared piner throwing herself aside. We plotted a past for her: meadow hockey in college, weddings called off, devotions forever obsolescing. We left a brood of brazen tulips on her doorstep. Pictured her kicky and ambitious sleep, an exercise of caution in her days, her vague but chaoticized dailiness. We started eating where she ate— ordered the same boffo salads, with just scribbles of onion, parings of radish fillipped in just right.

Still, we made no grabs, no gains, until my sister wondered, Maybe *we* were the couple?

What at first doesn't sit right might eventually be made to stand at least to reason.

•

Then came crackdowns at work—freezes on travel, on "favors" for office affairs. I liked how things got worded on the stop orders, and I liked how a day harshened around ten o'clock and again about three; I liked personal bombshells— the miscarriages and surprisingly affordable addictions.

But I mostly liked feeling pinned down, sized up, *taken* for.

The new guy they paired me off with was just some kid, formerly rural, with a headful of unmastered mathematics and specialty jests.

He figured in my toilet ruminations, true, but only as someone spooked, not spooking.

•

The library girl had the disease in its early, bashful stage. "Watch and wait," she said the doctors had said. But it did not come out of its shell the little while I knew her.

I would help her off with her coat, and she would put everything she had into a practiced shakiness that could not be ignored. The money we threw around was mostly money torn most of the way down the middle.

She had a diary she decorated alertly but wrote in only here and there—tidings, updates, mostly flashily inaccurate. I know because I, too, tended to peek at life and generally save my breath.

•

Then a boxier month holding more than I knew what to do with. My mother died idly and lopsidedly in her sleep, and within days had begun her cindered foray into the infinite. My father threw himself truantly into grieving, claimed he could hear his mind clearing up too soon. My older sister had started courting some galled dab of a man. He kept his back to the rest of us while we whiled away the days of bereavement pay.

This was supposed to be broad-skyed autumn, don't forget.

Slants were falling all across my life, too. A sore, a lasting blemish of some sort, had asserted a fresh residency on my chin.

Then my older sister had a change of heart, married her man's grappling brother instead. The ceremony was swift, inventive, isolating.

•

A year or two of slower considerings, and then another year broke out its days. I was newly forty, and veinier, but now and then still had a crack at people.

I squibbed myself this way and that into a few more women, fled the coming fruitions.

Then Elek.

I had known him for only the hour, but he left that scathing of citrus on my lips.

•

In years to come, I shared a house—some plywooden, hideaway housing, really—with a much younger woman who had a daughter, a keeper, from a man who had left. This woman and I helped each other off with high-collared sweaters that verged nearly to our shins, ate take-out pizzas that had been rechristened to sound like sensible dishes. We fought like equals. When the daughter grew up a little further and started overdoing it (she had a finessed, triumphal bloom on her), the two of them got mistaken for sisters wherever they went. They took to explaining that they were just good friends with hopes of someday being something more.

PEOPLE WON'T KEEP

~~Like everyone else in that kindergarten, I was told to bring
something from home to kill a couple of minutes in show-
and-tell. I brought in the one toy I'd been living for—a toy
drive-in theater. (Tiny cars, tiny snack bar, a tiny projector
that beamed film-stripped cartoons onto a tiny screen.)~~

~~A girl in the class cried out that the thing was hers.~~

~~The teacher, a Miss Somebody Else, naturally took her
part, handed the whole works over to the girl.~~

~~That quick, there was every way for me to go about not
rising in the world.~~

~~And in high school? I girled myself around the boys
retiring behind their guitars.~~

~~I enjoyed their entertainment of their every doubt.~~

~~Then college, and more college, then pointless turnabouts
between turning points.~~

~~Wife number one was always a baby at the table.~~

~~She came from that side of humanity that fostered a fern
on every stick of furniture.~~

~~She called her mother day in and day out, doing things to
her voice that made her sound uprooted.~~

~~Her mother's voice: "I want you to do something for me. I
want you to stretch your right arm out as far as it will go."~~

~~My wife's voice: "Okay."~~

~~Her mother: "Are you doing it? Are you up against
anything?"~~

~~My wife: "The back of a sofa."~~

Her mother: "Slap it so I can hear it's really there."

I forget if it was an alderman or a magistrate who served me with the papers. It looked like legerdemain.

Fair enough, but the next one I followed night after night to the locale's movie house, and sat in the same fusty dark through sentimental documentaries about fatal but honest mistakes. I shopped in the shop where she bought her rosy soda. (I pictured her, to a certainty, meekening it with tap water.)

She looked even more unmingleable with people than I: night-eyed and sofa-ridden and grimed, I supposed, from stinkhole recreations and the blunts of dumbing employments—nothing new pooling in her heart, and a wayside tendency to let things just pale, and that reigning voice of hers growing more professive by the mouthful when the subjects must have gotten touchier.

Thus: sudden kisses in her car, smushy and considerate at first. Then into her apartment, onto her husky furniture. (Only a daybed, though, with throws instead of sheets, the toilet muttering until morn.) We would run down a day in the solid clarity of the town, hold only the most lulling of things against each other. Such a rushed and rubbishing month! (Later, of course, all that mending talk, and the perspectival protection it probably should have brought.)

It turned out to be a commodious enough marriage, though. Other people started cropping up in it. They fell asleep on us, entertained our touch, cut us in on their injuries, their every setback and deadlock.

Then went away, to a man, so much the slower of heart.

This wife and I took to styling more and more feeling into our morning farewells.

We were believers, the two of us, in giving people their dwindling due.

Just the same, you learn to live without yourself.

You go behoovedly to work in safety pants.

But it's not you yourself who turns forty, forty-five, fifty—you *get* turned. *Dialed* forward and therefrom.

~~Except now I'm pushing, being pushed, sixty, with cataracts and suchlike. I listen through snow to the scrattle of a neighbor's shovel on the sidewalk out front.~~

~~There should be limits on how much can be spelled out on people.~~

The facts have yet to do their job.

I WAS IN KILTER
WITH HIM, A LITTLE

I once had a husband, an unsoaring, incompact man of forty, but I often felt carried away from the marriage. I was no childbearer, and he was largely a passerby, minutely berserk in his bearing. We had just moved to one of the little cities that had been set out at intervals—they formed a kind of loose oblong, I imagine—in the upper tier of our state.

He had an unconsoling side, this husband, and a mean streak, and a pain that gadded about in his mouth, his jaw, and there was a bumble of blond hair all over him, and he couldn't count on sleep, on dreams, to get a done day butchered improvingly.

He drove a mutt of a car and was the lone typewriter mechanic left in the territory, a servicer of devastated platens, a releaser of stuck keys.

I would let him go broadly and unseen into his day.

These cities each had a few grueling boulevards that urged themselves outbound. Buses passed from one city to the next and were kept conspicuously to their schedules, and I soon took to the buses, was taken with them: I would feel polite and brittle in my seat as a city was approached, neatened itself into streets and squares, then petered out again into bare topography. It never made much difference in which city I got off. I always had some business somewhere of a vaguely gracious, vaguely metropolitan sort, if only a matter of inquiring at a bank about exchanging some uncomely ones for a five. Sometimes I resorted to department stores, touched handbags, clutches (I have always preferred the undoing of any clasp); and I liked to favor a ladies' room with my solitude. I knew how to make an end of an afternoon, until the day lost pace and went choppy with a fineness I could refine the finality of.

It was mostly younger women on the buses—women barely clear of girlhood, dressed for functioning public loneliness in tarplike weighted cottons.

I one day sat down beside one.

My fingers were soon in the pan of her palm.

•

This city was a recent thing built in pious, cutback mimicry of someplace else. The streets were named after other streets.

I had been hired, probationally, as a substitute teacher, which meant I was not hated by any one student for any length of time, but I made enemies aplenty in the short haul.

I would write my name on the board, and then I would usually have one girl, a roupy-voiced thing, who would say, "Wait, I know you," and I would say, "I don't think so," and she would say, "Not from here."

Back in the practicums I had been taught to ask, "Who belongs to this paper?" Because you do run across cases where the possessory currents seem to be running more forcibly from the paper to the kid than the other way around. You're taught to feel something for anybody caught in that kind of pull, though I never once felt it.

I had, I hope, a dry, precise smile, a good-bye smile.

•

My husband: he had sized his life to deprive it of most of the right things.

I had been meaning to get something in here of our incensed domestic civility, and the queered quiet of our nights, and the preenings of the weather all the following summer, a summer that never cut either of us in on its havoc and seethe, but the mind's eye is the least reliable of the sightholes, and I might have been looking all along through only one of those.

It was availed away, our marriage.

We got tardier about every fresh start.

•

If I am talking them up again, these women brimming hectically now on buses, it can't be only to keep throwing pinched perspectives over their low points, every rut in their loveliness.

It's just that I tend to get all devotionate when I sense sore spots and unaired ires in any shrewd mess densening suddenly in my ken.

A Tuesday, for undiscouraged instance: a vexable, vapory girl.

My one hand mulling its way into a pocket of her coat.

(To join hers there at last.)

My other hand fluffing up the leg of her pants.

(The hair on her shin a chestnut-brown emphasis.)

I helped myself to their charity.

•

Ruthfully open arms, blind sides, always a general alcoholature to their breath—it was true a few of them might have been cautioning me all along to look out for myself, but I took that to mean what? That I was the fittest object of my own suspicions?

Women of muddled impulse, lonely beyond their means—I let my drowsy heart drowse around.

•

Then it was decided it was time to fix on just one of them. I was on a bus homeward from work. She was steadfast of face, and it was a situated face, or my idea of one, but her dress curtained her off so completely that the breasts were cryptic, the legs undefined.

Ideally, the way we sat, the way our forearms were set out in a line, her bracelet should have slid with ease from her wrist to mine. But the rumps of our hands were too thick to permit a crossing.

Then her apartment, a barracksy large, lone room: tenants on either side of us, and above, beneath, making overheard but unintelligible dead-set headway.

She had sweepy arms, a squall of dark hair, eyes a slubby brown. She spoke through prim, petite teeth of favors she was owed.

There was relief in how quick we could find the hardness in each other.

•

Then weeks, scrapes of inquisitive affection, kisses kept quiet and dry, unluminary movements not undear to me, a clean breast made here or there, every passing thought treated to a going explanation (people combine *unneatly*), an inaccurate accusation, a principal I had to have it out with.

They weren't hours, these classes; they weren't even forty-five minutes—they were "periods," which sounded to me as if they were each at once a little era and the end you had to see decisively put to it.

I would be summoned from school to school, grade to grade, and I would advance through a class, a subject, a unit, by picking on yet another nobody undergoing youth, and I would peer into her worried homeliness, let a trait or feature advocate itself for half an hour's discrediting endearment.

Eyes, maybe; eyes of a sticky green that looked fuddled with the world and its ongoing insistence that things, people, remain detailed and unalike.

Or an unblunt arm unsleeved in late autumn and within esteeming reach, though I had come to believe miserably in seeing arms not as the pathway to a person but as the route the body took to get as far afield of itself as it could.

Evidence pointed directly to other evidence, never directly to me. What influence did I have? I spoke from notes.

•

When you are no good at what you do, it does you no good to triumph at whatever you might come home to, either. My husband was in fact my second one. I should be making a case for the first, for the avenues of feeling I must have taken with him, though he mostly just roved from room to room between charley horses, was studious in his insults, twidged a slowpoke finger into where I still trickled against my will.

Let me remember him, at least, for being the one to teach me that there was only one polite way left to say "yes," and that was "I'm afraid so."

•

I am admittedly leaving out a kid I left eventually with an aunt, my one uncornering aunt, but I imagine I did later write a letter to be given to the kid when the kid finally aged overnight.

I wrote it in emotional accelerations of my pen on hotel stationery on an evening when the fitness of the word *evening* struck me for once, for isn't it the business of that first reach of the night to even out any remaining serrations of the day?

I was a woman heaping all alone into her thirties.

Things allowed me mostly lowered me.

•

My young woman, then: she was technically out of the nest, but there was a parent she reported to, and I must have known there were other goads.

In the nightlight, I could see where she had been C-sectioned. A weak grief usually strutted her up. She sometimes thumbed an hour aside with habits, practices; brought an abruptly feared finger down onto the pricket of a candleholder, maybe, to gloat over dribbleting blood. But the nail of the finger had been cheered an opera pink, or a mallow purple, and there was nothing uncourtly in her intonations.

I was thus kept milling in her feelings still.

For a living, she banged about tables in a downstairs restaurant scaled back now to only breakfast and a rushed late lunch. She would settle her stomach with formally forked portions of what had unsettled it in the first place.

But how best to be usefully afraid for her? I could never get a sense of where others might be perched in her affections.

Her name—I dare not draw it out here—was a huddle of scrunty consonants and a solitary vowel, short. I should have done a better job of learning how to say the thing without its getting sogged somehow.

•

A family? That was where you got crooked out of childhood.

I had been sixteen when I grew into my mother's size—an already tight and terrible ten. Our wardrobes overlapped for a while, then no longer got sorted at all. We would pick a day's dark attire out of the dryer, and had to go from there.

Or you could go back even further, to when you are barely untucked from childhood and finally get the full run of your body, and feel secure in all its workings, then learn that everything on it will now have to be put to dirtier purpose.

But my brother? I was in kilter with him, a little.

I turned on him, then turned back.

There was already wide plight to my tapering life.

•

One night, though, I had to use her bathroom. It was mostly men's things in there—shaving utilities, drab soaps, an uncapped deodorant stick with a military stink to it.

When I came out, the phone rang.

"Let it sleep," she said.

(The handset had, after all, a "cradle.")

Then later, someone slapping away at the door.

The slaps were all accumulating at one altitude at first, but then traveled unmightily down the door panel to the knob.

Then sudden, fretful turnings of the knob.

We listened, hands united, until the commotion at the door was a gone-by sound, followed by the gone-by sounds of feet in the hallway, then of a car entered, roused, driven expressively away.

•

Prescription oblivials gave her an assist with her moods, veered her toward a slow-spoken sociability sometimes, sometimes made her meaner.

We would sit down dearly to a dinner of whiskery import vegetables, close-cropped meat gone meek in the sauce, everything on side plates, everything a lurid obscurer of itself.

But why lie when the truth is that the truth jumps out at you anyway?

Before me, so she claimed, it had been a narrow-faced shopmaiden with a muggy bosom and a catastrophal slant to her mind.

To hear her tell it, there were girl friends (two words), there were girlfriends (one word), there were friend girls, and there were women. Women were never your friend.

•

Baby talk like that must have put the lacquer back onto my life for a while.

I stood up quite handsomely now to my husband's entire, perspirant heights.

One morning I thumbed out most of the teeth from a comb of his, stuck them upright in rough tufts of our carpet—whatever it then took to get a barefoot person hurt revolutionarily.

•

But the days arched over us and kept us typical to our era. It was an era of untidying succors, follied overhauls.

Her manager gave her more hours.

Her feelings came down to me now in just dwindlements of the original.

She started showing up in the snap judgments of a glass-blowing uncle, and was an aunt herself to two nieces already girthed and contrarious.

We had them over, those two, to her place, our table. They had been lured through youth with holiday slugs of liquor, had put themselves through phases but always stopped short of complete metamorphosis.

The younger was the more bridelike. Skewy eyes, a dump of dulled hair. A sparge of moles on the neck, the shoulder.

The older's shoe kept knocking against my own.

She picked a hole in her biscuit, didn't seem to have any tides dragging at her.

They each later took me aside to tell me what they had had the nerve to collect, study, and forsake. Thick books read to detriment; tiny, frittery animals—need I say?

Afterward, the woman and I alone, the night gone quickly uninfinite: I kept seizing things—household motes and the like—out of the broad, midbody bosh of her hair.

But if I say I felt something for her, would that make it sound as if I felt things in her stead, bypassing her completely?

Because that might too be true.

•

When you're a renter, a tenant, an apartment-house impermanent, you make do without cellarways, attics, crawl spaces: there's little volume your life can fill.

So you take it outside to the open air—into *thin* air, you've already corrected yourself.

The eye doctor started calling my husband a "glaucoma suspect." There were drops and a dropper on the nightstand, pamphlets of attenuated portent.

I got better at tugging away the context from around every least thing. Something as unchaotical, I mean, as the compact she had suddenly stopped caring for. It no longer made the daily dainty descent into her purse.

I got alone with it, unclamped the clamshell casing.

Spoofed much too much of its powder onto my nose, my cheeks.

Waited.

Waited even longer.

No alarms to report then and there, of course, but I must have, ever after, felt eaten away a little more around the clock.

•

My weeks with this bare woman dipped deficiently toward winter. She either worried herself back into my attentions, or a day got minced into minutes we just wished away. Her love for me, in short, was a lopsided compliment, longer in the rebuke than in the glorifying.

(The freshest snow on the streets already grooved and slutted by traffic.)

•

Another night of roundabout apologizing, and she reached for a shoulder bag, not one of her regular daytime totes. She tipped it all out, fingered everything preservingly where it fell.

The whole business was already looking a little too votive to me.

First the smoot, the flaked razures and other collects, that she had abstracted from the gutter between blades of an overemployed disposable shaver. (It had taken, she said, the corner edge of an index card to reclaim this richesse.)

Then, in a mouth-rinse bottle, a few fluidal ounces of sea-blue slosh from a compress that had been used whenever there were immaculate agonies behind a knee.

And a smutched inch or so of adhesive tape from a homemade bandage, into which pores had confided their oily fluences. All stickage had long gone out of the thing. (She draped it inexactly across her wrist.)

It had all been her sister's, she said, if a sister is who it had been.

I am always in doubt of whoever can't die right away.

•

She was gone some nights, too. Things happen when you are younger and have it in you to pinpoint your satisfactions.

I would take the bus to look in on my husband. In my absence, life had scarcely scratched at the man. He never bothered going through my pockets or sought secrets in my miscellaneals. His point of view was exactly that—a speck, something too tiny to even flick away. We were in the bathroom; he was razoring the daily durations of hair from his cheeks, his chin. I was sitting shiftily along the brim of the tub. There was the hankering hang of his thing. I let it fool itself out to me.

•

Days were not so much finished as effaced. You caught sight of new, unroomy hours looming through the old. Then months more: months of fudging forward unfamished. Then a Sunday night, a worldly evening, finally.

We got off the bus, the woman and I, at the first town we came to. It was a paltry locality with a planetarium, a post office, a plaza. The plaza had a restaurant. We went in, ordered, raked through each other's romaine, thinned out the conversation, set off for the restroom together. Somebody had taped to the mirror a reminder that hands should be washed for thirty seconds—the exact length, the sign went on to say, of a chorus of "Happy Birthday." We thus sang as we soaped the other's dickering fingers, but when we came within syllables of the end of the third line, where you have to put in the name of the "dear" celebratee, we broke things off.

It was the same driver for the trip back—not a nice man.

This being my history, I snapped out of my marriage, pieced myself back into the population, prodded and faulted, saw red, then wed anew in wee ways.

This husband and I soon set a waning example of even our own business.

I later fell in with a girl who kept a cat on her head to stay warm.

I was mostly of a mood to pollute, and she was frank in her dreams, which she logged, but a liar in all other opportunities.

Then years had their say.

HEARTSCALD

HOME

When I got back from the mall, everything in my room had been rotated almost a whole eighth of an inch to the right.

I am taping it all back into place.

FEMALE VOICE ON PHONE: "NO MORE CONTACT"

I can't speak for myself, but a job does things to a person, deducts a person pretty brutally from life.

Desks are terrible places, no matter how many wheels a chair might have.

You can't do much about how drawers fill up.

WHAT TO DO WITH THE OHIO RIVER

Drain it, obviously.

Hire me to walk its length and gloat.

PLACE-NAMES

I once thought Ave Maria was one.

NEIGHBORS

He slips a note under my door, says he has forgotten how to talk, so is there something that can be done?

I meet him in the lobby. I bring my instruments in a wastebasket.

"It's my first time," I warn.

I go to work on him.

His first words: "I've got something in my eye. A kingdom or something."

ERRAND

The girl behind the counter rang up my package of paper towels and said, "Will that be all?"

"No," I said. "I want to suck out all of your memories."

THE TROUBLE BETWEEN PEOPLE USUALLY GETS ITS START

The pastor kept saying, "Thy will be done," and all I could think was, "Thy *what* will be done?"

I USED TO LOVE LPs

I used to love carrying them home from the store, the big, goofy flatness of the things.

I thought the numbers parenthesized after the song titles were letting you in on the time of day when the songs had been taped.

I thought the peak time for singers, bands, orchestras, was between 2:30 and 3:30.

LIKE THE LADY IN THE PLAY,

I have always depended on the strangeness of my kind.

SHE WAS CARDIACALLY ALL OVER THE PLACE

What they told me is that when the doctors opened him up, they found lots of accordion files, jars full of wheat pennies, a glockenspiel, a couple of storm windows, and told him there was nothing they could do.

RECORD PLAYER

I used to play my records with the volume turned all the way down.

I would lower my ear to the needle to hear the tiniest, trebliest versions of the songs.

I AM AWFULLY FOND OF THE INTERNET

Trouble is, I hang on its every word. I have old-fashioned, home-style dial-up that entitles me to seven screen names. I've finally curbed my online activity by using the "parental controls," which I exercise by means of intricate settings from my primary screen name. The controls allow me to set restrictions on the nature and duration of the Internet activity conductable under each of the other six names. So for each of them I've permitted myself exactly one hour of activity each day, but it's a different hour each day for each screen name, and unless I log on during that one hour, I'm out of luck. There's no way, of course, that I can remember the allowable hour for each name for every day of the week, and I naturally never bothered to write any of it down. The result is that most of the time I can't get onto the Internet at all, and it would be much too much trouble to go back and undo all the settings. So you might say, "Well, then, do all your business—whatever that might be, and it can't be all that ennobling if you've gone and placed so many obstructions in your path—from your primary screen name." Yes, yes, very good point, but somehow the Internet access from my primary screen name seems clogged, or something.

WORK

My humanity would have been misemployed no matter what direction I might have taken in life, but, no question, I have walked away cravenly from blocked-up photocopiers, paper jams of any kind.

A lot of toner has gone into all I have done.

THERE WERE WIDER AND WIDER SLITS IN A DAY

She had a three-legged table.

I always felt bad about that.

THE WHOLE DAY WAS TOSSING AHEAD OF HIM

As is generally the case, the father's love for his daughter was sporadic and awful.

The town's founders could have done a better job of laying things out so everything wouldn't be within a stone's throw.

I have to go around her to get anywhere.

GIRL

She wanted me to believe her best feature was her shadow.

PEOPLE KEPT OPENING WIDE

I keep seeing the phrase "a women" everywhere I look.

Trouble is, it can't be just a typo anymore.

SECOND WIFE

The human body is far too hot.

It cooks things right out of your heart.

CESAREAN

I was hired to pack the old kind of computer disks into boxes for mailing, or maybe they weren't even computer disks, because this might have been longer ago than that.

The supervisor said, "Just make sure you ball up some newspaper into every box to pad it." He pointed to stacks and stacks of old papers banked against a wall.

Later, he checked in on me. Most of the papers were gone.

He picked up a box, then another, and another.

"Why the hell are these so heavy?"

FIRST WIFE

I don't know which is finally sicker—specifics or engulfing abstractions.

She said she was just looking for someone to ride out some sadness on.

MOTHER AND BANGED-UP SON

Looking back over everything I might have ever said, I see that I have never come down hard enough on any of the rooms I lived inside.

I want there to be science behind it if and when I do.

FATHERLAND

The state I was born in had to be abbreviated as "Pa."

HONOR MY WISH

I tried drinking, but it wasn't extinctive of the parts of me most in need of extinction. Plus, I had a good umbrella, but it got blown inside out, and I couldn't get the thing to close. I set it down on the sidewalk and watched it blow off into the storm.

I welcome any drowsy and senseless sincerity.

I COULD SEE WHERE SHE WAS STUCK

A man I knew had had car trouble for years. He got around by bus.

He had just the one daughter, and I knew what she needed to be told.

I could feel the words already forming into solids in my head: *There's no such thing as parents.*

When the time came for her to go off to college, she picked one in the state that was shaped far too much like the human heart.

She arrived at the airport seven hours ahead of her flight.

The automatic doors that led from the long-term parking lot to the terminal wouldn't even open for her. She tried all three sets of them. The sensors, she guessed, failed to detect sufficient bodily or characterical presence.

She should have brought luggage, school supplies, a change of underattire.

An untroubled-looking couple turned up.

The doors parted.

She rushed in behind.

SECOND WIFE

We had to move two towns to the left, which was west, westish, in this case.

GIRL

I was singing over petite chords fingered on an electric guitar that wasn't plugged in.

It was a song of infatuation that I eventually passed along to the infatuatee. She said the chorus could use a little something more to fill it out.

My voice was as flat as it ever gets.

It sounded practically ventriloquized.

I'M AFRAID I AM NOTHING SO DEAR

The hours keep dragging things out of us or throwing us into reunion.

I want everything elegized the instant it happens.

MY LIFE TAKES PLACE MOSTLY ON THE FLOOR

"Get over here!" I shouted into the phone.

The woman came.

She thought I had meant just her.

THIS IS NOT WHAT I WANTED TO SAY, BUT SO WHAT?

I wish I could inhabit my life instead of just trespassing on it.

I LATER SUFFERED ATTRACTION TO SOMEONE A LITTLE LESS LIKE HER

There should be a way for this to go straight into my short-term memory.

There should be buttons to press, entire consoles of buttons.

This should be more like science fiction and less like hate, pure and simple.

PULLS

It has always been my custom to go hungry for people, then make my way practically from door to door. But there was a time I had a wife and a new best friend.

I was just doing the weary thing of being in my forties.

My wife wanted to be known best for her parting shots, the breadth of her good-byes. I could count on her to be back within hours, though, tidily silent in her chair.

And the best friend? He was an uncrusading man, rebuttable in everything. He looked felled, or probably at least fallen.

I began dividing my nights between them.

•

This wife and I had a rented house, two storeys of brutal roomth. The air conditioner required a bucket underneath it. Our meals were the cheapest of meats thinly veiled.

My best friend had some uncovetable rooms above a garage. We took down hours with our talk.

•

Here's her name—Helene—though she will probably tell you different.

•

For a while, I tried to get her steered toward women. We settled on a blowhard of sporty despondence, crude to the eye but newly starving for her own sex. I staked the two of them to a meal and threw in good wishes.

She came home ebbing in all essences, looking explored and decreased.

She wanted to know about my best friend. I told her that he and I fell onto each other more in sexual pedantry than out of affection, that our life together did not grow on us or chew away at our hearts. His body was just profuse foolery.

Thirty-eight years of picked-over, furying age she was—brittled hair, a bulwark forehead, a voice that sounded blown through. There were hidey-holes in whatever she said.

I felt indefinite inside of her, out of my element and unstately in my need.

•

One night he wanted to know what it had been like to go through with the nuptials, the hymeneals. Not much had held up in memory. I let out that the minister had spoken of a "middle ground" between women and men or husband and wife, I forget—someplace irrigated and many-acred, maybe a plain. I had felt unchampioned that day. The minister got me alone at the reception, snapped his fingers, said, "This better not've been just some skit."

•

There are only two things, really, to ever say to anyone.

Try: "I'm very happy for you."

Or: "This is just not done."

•

I made no more than the arcanest of passes at others. They probably never even knew they had been addressed or beset. I worked for a sloganless bail-bond concern. The people closest to me in seating were a rough-playing woman and a man about my age, drowning in the hours. The woman drank liquored sodas that brought something flowerful into her voice: words were now petally with extra syllables. The man took a restroom break whenever he saw somebody else come out. Maybe he found something engreatening about being in there so soon after anything dirtily human had been done. I pictured him taking deep, treasuring breaths, filling up on us. Home was probably just an air mattress somewhere.

I lived in the lonelihold of my portents and pulls.

•

Weeks kept fleeting past us.

My wife restocked her mind daily with factual packing from TV and the papers.

I would want a day to quit. Thinking what, though? That the one rising behind it might have a more encouraging bone structure in its hours or at least be calibered better for my regrets?

•

Then one night she wanted to know how she might recognize my friend on the street.

I spoke of the ordering of creases above his eyes, the general tempo of both his blinks and his nostril-flarings, the pitch and range of his arms, the usual drift of the rib that slid about inside him.

But nothing eased for her or for me.

•

My parents were still alive, still short on marvelry, still saying, "We're all he has."

I had a sister, too, drying out again in the tedium of debt somewhere.

She was an acher, patient but baneful in her morbid sweats.

I thus sing the praises of my kind, but more often I just look for signals in the faces of grocery cashiers who are required to say "hi"—women mostly, overevident in their agony; features miseried, it must be, by hitches in the upbringing of their men.

•

We tried pets, my wife and I. Bought a dog at cost, then a budget cat.

The dog was unawed by my guidance, my sweet talk.

The cat behaved—out of a love or regard, though, that was iotal, toiling.

If you bought for one, you had to buy for the other. (Mostly novelties to squeeze for a spectral, unmerry squeak.)

I wish I could remember whether they bailed on us or just died, overfed.

•

Another generation had shot up behind us anyway.

I had heard about these persons—that they were handling things differently.

This was the generation that was discovered to have been "just reading words" and then was taught how to get through a textbook by coloring the sentences so that a page, when the fingers had finished with it, looked beribboned, or zoned into chromatic blocks and runs. The books were handed in to the teacher, who graded mostly on pizzazz.

Nothing went untouted about these kids.

I went out and found one at a shopping center.

She was aimless of face, but things had been staged in her hair—demonstrations of metal and feather in the low altitudes of stickied coralline. What she wore wasn't so much a cover as a kind of kiting, blown about before her as she thugged away at a mood. Whims of string (from a shoe, I think) were ringed around her wrist.

She had just been graduated from the two-year institute outside of town.

I took her out for one of the current coffees.

She asked whether I knew that cold water melted ice cubes faster than hot.

I nodded learnedly.

She mentioned "sleeping in."

I told her I had been well into my central twenties before it dawned on me that to "sleep with" someone didn't simply mean to take a companion for your horizontal hours and thereby get sleep domed over you so much the higher than it would if you went home to bed alone. I had thought that was how you gave greater compass, greater volume, to your dreams.

She sipped, and shook her head, and said sleep roamed all over her—it was tramply; it left reddening trackage on her back.

"Not that you'll ever get to see," she said.

She wanted my address anyway. I gave her the friend's. I did get one letter later, a good-bye. It was, she wrote, a "bill adieu."

•

I am leaving out the hobbies, the odd jobs, the aplomb I had that just got harder and harder on people.

But I will admit I went to the doctor about the ache in my face. It eventually swelled my cheeks and slit into my sleep.

The doctor called it a "referred" pain. It had arrived, he claimed, from someplace else.

He shunted me off to a specialist, who said the body always waits until the last minute to explain itself to you.

•

And my wife? I had borne some of the brunt of her fresh starts, seen what helping hands could do with someone like that.

Even her arm—the flesh of it looked tilled, perfected in every lurid turning away. It could withstand scrutinies more spiteful than mine.

She fell in with a man full of biblical quips, brash intelligence about the presaging capers of his Lord. I saw her vivified and steep by his side in the business district one day. I was by myself in the house every other night. I liked the reliable isolations. I spent some time in the book she had been through. There had been obvious violence in her sessions with it. The binding was loose. It barely had a clutch on the leafage anymore. The bookmark kept sliding out.

She came back to me with tiny growths in her groin and a new, striving vagueness of eye.

•

Then I found a huge laundry room in an apartment tower near the house. For a time, I couldn't do enough laundries there. Nobody caught on that my basket was practically empty. I would enchant every machine with dollar-store detergent, then get the things gushing and thumping through their cyclicals.

I confined myself to one item per load. This ensured a cautious, tyrannical clean.

Even better, there was a lost-and-found, a big cardboard box torn down a little from the top. I started bringing things to kick in—whatever clamored up toward me from the lowest of my life. The thinking must have been that I was most devoted to people I had not yet met, that I was best at laying out courtesies in advance. Thus the box filled mostly with helpings from my wardrobe: shirts gathering further shine; slacks that were negligences of hemmed fabric, down whose twinned chutes my legs had once gone their separate ways.

•

My best friend and I were now living in an underhanded familiarity that, from farther off, might have been taken for an advance in attachment.

We made it to the yard sales and brought back further caprices of the culture. Once it was just a mug whose hectic lettering said, "READ A MAGAZINE TONIGHT!"

But nothing much was flaring in my heart.

One night I told him that our lives differed in unbeautifying ways. I told him our bodies could never really be in league.

I pointed at his hand. It had just left mine and was started on its way elsewards.

His fingers always looked as if they were squabbling among themselves, undecided about what might next be deserving of touch.

•

My wife was walking a fine line, wearing herself away from me.

Months broadened in their burden.

Then the advent of her scandal: sprigs of intimate hair trapped, specimenized, in the clear sealing tape all over the holiday packages that went out one noon to "influentials." Her defense? Anything hailing from a body had to be worthy of at least flitting reverence on your way to the sink.

But cracks had started forming in her words. Things ever after were fissured in her speech.

·

Then the girl wanted to see me after all. Told me to meet her in the new wing of the closest mall. There was a swinge of ambition in her step as she saw me drawing near.

She hated all her friends now, she said—preeners mostly, demanding dripling sorrows of every instant in her shadow. And what about me? she wondered. Did people my age have friends?

I mentioned a couple of people who lifted emotions without giving credit yet expected originality in any affections coming from me.

"Tell me your wife's side," she said.

·

One evening, I caught sight of a man who had assumed himself anew in my slacks, my shirt, my jacket and shoes.

He was startleproof in some sort of painless hurry, apparently.

The look he gave me was not a grateful one, or even salutatious, but I felt at large.

·

One night the three of us were in our right minds around the same table. There might have been a birthday. I remember that something consolatory had been ciphered into the icing of a store-baked cake.

I grabbed her hand.

Released its fingers—or set them out, rather, in severalizing meander—onto his arm.

I must have thought I was getting something exalted on one or the other.

The fingers, I could see, were stuck.

I got up, feeling scanted and surpassed.

My life now dates from that day.

YOU'RE WELCOME

Worse, I had been the husband, most recently, of a sweetly unpoised, impersonal woman, and in the months following the divorce (it would not have been worth the bother of an annulment, she had said; annulments were reserved for circumstances even more gloriously unfornicatory than ours), I had been getting sicker and sicker of living in conclusion in the little riverless city to which I had always returned after any kind of body blow or setback to my likelihood. But the divorce somehow didn't feel finished to me, I didn't feel riddled with it, or partitioned any farther from her; and having learned, from some florid passersby, that she was living in lower Europe with an aunt or an uncle with small sprouts of money, or sponging off somebody at least welcomingly kindred, I crossed the ocean to see what else there could be that might extinguish what I felt persisted between the two of us. There had to be a surer way to consummate the end of things already ended.

I was a stare-about on the nightlong flight, pacing the aisles, pushing aside every meal and snack, hogging the lavatory for half-hours at a time, thinking that my thinking was, "You don't want to go over it again, how you go from being a part to being apart." And how true, for marriage had given us the chance to cultivate our mussed lonelinesses shoulder to shoulder, my lunatic of a penis uncoaxable into even the simplest of bedstead sex.

People were plugged up enough as it was.

We—*I*—landed at length in some city not even worth my putting the stony name to it here, because I wouldn't want anyone feeling envious that I, of all tossed-aside American males, had made such a crossing, especially since from the instant I put myself out onto via this and rue that, I paid the place no mind, took in none of the sights, ate only in the hamburger hideouts of tourists afraid of their own shadow. The hotel was a questionable piece of work, nothing like my apartment, that seventh heaven of meds and stink bugs, where my dreams either sneaked from sore point to sore point or beat me to a pulp.

It was a couple of days until I met up with her in some plaza or other. There was a man with her almost terribly.

"Maybe you should go take in the town for just a bit," she said to him. He dropped back, the way people commonly did around her.

Her bare arms swung boldenly as we walked to some kind of bistro. A utopian diet had limited her to rigorisms of tofu, but I ate a smattering of bacon and toast. I could tell she was stirring words inside of herself, and then she and I talked over each other about what we had coming to us, every tit for tat of it, reparations conceivably computable. Her gut had always told me everything: that there are many kinds of love, but ours had never been one of them. Need I have reminded myself, then, of the times I had moved around on her, drudged from an underarm to the rear of a knee, but always stopped short of anything that would put me across as someone connubially constituted for a woman so beautied to the point where you had to wonder whether she had ever been beautiful at all? The marriage had been no time to start.

Her face, scarcely tended to with a scamble of blush, had assimilated some heavily haphazard eyeglasses. (The frames, new to me, looked as if hewn from rock.) But she struck me as not uncomely, if a trifle overhauled, her hair supplemented now, her dress an affluence of daylight-blue tugged over breasts looking newly punched up.

My own body—dare I drag the thing in here?—had been exacted baggily over an inner nature unrooted-for and undelighting. I couldn't break free from any of this body's leakages or procedures.

But her eyes, as ever, went vagrant when she talked. Her life was better now, she said. People went easier on her. Even the ones who had it in for her had to hand it to her that she was good at what she was doing, even (I gathered) if all she was doing was gauding about coolly in falsehoods extraordinaire.

"What about you?" she said. "What are the love interests? Let's hear of their displeasing miseries one by one."

I said that people tended to get dislocated when I touched them too much. I stretched things too far.

"Nonsense," she said. "You don't put yourself out there at all."

I took out my wallet and showed her a photo of a woman who had long ago taken refuge in a haven of a sweater many sizes too immense. She looked hardly even noticeable in the picture. But in point of fact she was a skin-and-bones difficulty with arrhythmic outages of affection and a butchery of blue-black hair. She had tapped me, variously, pandemoniacally, for kindliness and money, but then started offering us, as a couple, to others. In no time, people, bamboozlers themselves, had gone through us just to get through with us.

"Who left whom," my ex-wife said—as a reminder, though, and not as a question.

Wine she wanted now. The afternoon had issued itself quarter-hour by quarter-hour into buggy evening, a drizzle-drozzle so soon on the windows.

She was claiming to be pregnant in some desultory way or another. She said she had been having a devil of a time with it. She asked me to ask the waiter if he knew of any old hand at abortion. The waiter had that look of contented demolishment you often see over there. He wore a skirty apron and narrowy shoes, slippers almost, and spoke to us as if straight from his private life. He led us to the front of the place and pointed across the way to an arcade of sorts.

We held hands in a pedal-taxi on the little passage over. I felt derisions of warmth in her palm.

The abortioner's office was at the back of a machine shop and was full of swatters, plumb bobs, toilet plungers. This was a staminal man with dinky eyes and fingers that kept niggling at each other as he spoke. On an ironing board behind him: a midget computer, bluey and ablip.

"This is the wife-in-chief?" he said.

A funny way to put it, because I figured we had always been equals in whatever was most petty or fruitless at the moment. But you had to factor in her tendencies to entice and deprive.

"I am in want of an opinion," she said.

"Remove all wraps, trimmings, fixings," he said to her.

"No reason for you to leave," he said to me.

"I never left," I said.

"I meant now," he said.

She unbuttoned, unzipped. I had forgotten, I suppose, the finely hirsute earthliness of her, that vicious uneternal splendency. (The skelter of moles along the small of her back, the salmon-patch birthmark on the nape of her neck, the bubbly something near the groin—that droll, brazen sincerity of her body had always been a sticking point.)

He reached for a whisklike thing, then something along the lines of an awl. Proddled and poked into her a little. Then, after a clinical minute or so, said to her: "Somebody has been pulling your leg. You're not up to anything at all in there."

He pointed unclemently to me.

"Maybe it's him it's inside," he said. "Maybe I should be scraping around in your man there."

"He's not my man," she said.

"How long not?"

"Over a year now. Closer to two," she said. "I'm with somebody else."

"It takes a lot longer in a man, though. It goes unclocked."

Then: "But just look how crammed the guy looks. Look how chockablock that gut."

"We were against having kids," she said.

"This won't be a kid," he said.

And to me: "Desert what you're wearing."

I did as I was told. Stripped—or, rather, felt things tearing, being torn, away from me. If it's hard to say, it's because of my hands, the way each of them had always been contrary to the nature of the other.

"Your heart is jerking," he said.

All I knew was that I was naked, skeptical, ill-spun, beastly, muddlesome, shame-burnt, dashed and thankless, disheveled in every sinew. (I had always preferred my body sight unseen.)

It was a plastic hanger, not one of the wire ones, he finally came at me with. He hooked the thing into my behind and pulled and pulled educatedly until he let out a peep that just as soon structured itself downward an octave or two until it was harrumph after harrumph of chronic expertise.

"You keep yourself awfully stocked," he said.

He exchanged the hanger for a shower-curtain rod.

Ripped into me again.

Fetched out, and set down on the plane of the ironing board, the expectable barrettes, compacts, lipsticks, and atomizers, but also:

- the serpentinous leathern strap of a shoulder bag (clips included);
- pages wrung from a scratch pad with what must have been phone numbers scribbled over until they were gibberished into inconsultable, unconsolatory faces blurrily girly;
- airline-boarding-pass envelopes, stuffed with an overkill of nervily plucked coils of bikini-line hair;
- receipts for shoes of synthetic materials only, for fair-trade coffee beans, the receipts a little smeary, as if having blotted the oils from the tip of a much finer nose;

- a head-shot photo, scissored from a magazine, of some sacked sit-com actress, taken to salons as a prompt for the stylist to age her just so (bangs, featherings, tints);
- a ropy noose of a necklace in full, but just smashments of chokers, lockets, bangly teakwood—

"That's it?" the man said. He stepped back, the better to hurl the curtain rod at me. "That's the most trouble you've gone to?"

He called me a man of pronenesses instead of convictions, screamed things even more coring, threatened my life, walked me out to the tram to see me off, etc.

I forget if she was still with me then or not.

•

This isn't all of it, obviously, just some notes I must have taken not much later, overstepping. I had never been the type of man that women reassessed. I do know that in days to come I heard that she and the man had gotten themselves thrown out of her aunt and uncle's, or whomever's, and were living in a bed-and-breakfast in the same ruin-heaped city, and I liked to think that they were going to have to feel it in their bones just as I had always felt it in hers—that lingering business, I figured, about fitting new people and their irritable parts to the old feelings, the feelings that only made you feel as if you were going to have to get permission to chalk any of it entirely up to her.

Life—mine, I mean—might best be left unattended.

TIC DOULOUREUX

My brother and I were the last of the sons still living at home. It was my aunt's job—once a month a pay envelope was propped against a step halfway up the staircase—to see to it that I was kept some distance from him. One afternoon she told me to drop what I was doing and walk with her to the room in which he was kept. I trailed her down the hall as far as the doorway, then stopped.

"No monkey business," my aunt said.

The room was dark and windowless. This was still very early in ragweed season, and my brother was the only one of us the pollen had wanted much to do with. Handkerchiefs were balled up on his bare chest and on the floor beside the footage of yellowed foam rubber on which he was taking his slumbers. There had to be so many handkerchiefs, I was tired of being told, because a single one would have been soppy, draggled, useless, in no time.

"Go ahead," my aunt said.

I seized each handkerchief by the corner and shook it out into a lank spookling and then passed it along to my other hand until I had a dank fraternity of at least a dozen or so of the things squirming together.

My aunt started toward the doorway.

"Go," she said. Her eyes, I could see, were watering a trifle.

In my room, I dunked the handkerchiefs one by one into the scummed water in the wash pail and, without rinsing or wringing, distributed them across the floor to dry. At some point, I composed myself—stretched myself out atop the handkerchiefs to cool the backs of my legs. I pictured, as always, the gleaming expanse of my brother's chest, smooth as tile. I might have fallen part of the way asleep.

Every room on our floor was a complete dwelling, with something to fall asleep upon, and a wash pail, and another pail for whatever was going to desert our bodies, and something to cover the food we never could finish.

When you are one age, my father was fond of repeating, practically anything is either a blanket or a bed, no matter what it might have started out to be. But I was no longer that age.

•

I one day entered a room where my aunt had got ahold of a newspaper. She was trying to find a reliable way to keep a taut double-page of it aloft, kite-like, between outstretched arms. She shoved it at me.

"Read this and tell me what you get out of it," she said.

There was an article about the different things people ate and wore in a different part of the world. It was padded with recipes and sewing patterns, anecdotes, excitant quotes. I could see how old and rotten the thing was. I gave my aunt a chunked, inaccurate summary.

"Nothing in there about brothers?" she said. "How brothers should behave themselves around each other?"

She reclaimed the paper, tried to get it up in the air again.

"It names all the places they're allowed at on each other," I said. "It names everything about the places."

"Show me where it says any such thing," she said. "They can't print that in a paper."

I stabbed my finger through the page, jerked it out of her hands. I returned to the tropical stink of my room and counted the number of times my brother at the other end of the house sneezed next in succession—forty and seven.

•

Downstairs, it was a regular house. My parents were partners in a failing sales venture that confined them to hotels for weeks on end, but when they came back, their voices rose up through the hardwood floors, reminding us to mind our teeth or running over the details of turning points, of showdowns, with finicking clients. We were expected to make our reactions, our acknowledgments that we had heard, sufficiently audible. Sometimes I just pounded on the floor. My brother often followed this example. I could tell when he was using his elbows and not his fists, because with an elbow you do not get nearly as much thud. The sound is more pointed. A few times I heard the ball of a bare foot. Once I swear I made out what had to have been his skull. There was nothing from his direction for a long while after that, so I drummed enough for the two of us, moving about in the room and out into the hallway, but whom was I fooling?

During my parents' absences we were permitted downstairs no more than twice a day—one at a time, my aunt first—to choose our food and to fetch our water for drinking and dousing. We emptied our pails in the powder room. The toilet had a new seat that was not screwed on properly. It would slide out from beneath you unless you knew the right way to sit. The sink had no stopper, so you had to make sure there was nothing loose on you or on your smock when you bent forward to wash. Only one burner on the stove was even hooked up. There was a wagon-wheel-like chandelier above the kitchen table, which had an extension-leaf slid into it. One afternoon I sat at the table with a dish my mother had covered with foil in the refrigerator. It held a fantastication of stringy meat overextended with cake crumbs and edged with vegetabular sliverings that didn't quite sit right. I happened to hear my brother squishing along the floor upstairs in socks that must have still been soaking wet. That day I began to develop an appreciation for how things upstairs sounded to people underneath. From every footfall, every stride, came a creak that rippled outward until it overspread the entire ceiling of the room. The effect was one of resounding activity, of achievements far and wide.

•

"If it'll get your mind off it," my aunt said.

She had disposed herself beneath me, her eyes already shut, her hair a leaden bulk, an infrequent twinkle in her fingernails.

I filled her body with some pulse of my trouble. From the window I could make out the low-roofed town, untrafficable in the haze. One of the housetops close by was handsomely slated and slick. I slid my mind onto it for a clammy duration.

This is what days were now like in the morning if I hoped to see my brother come afternoon.

•

My heyday was the week or so my brother and I were finally boyfriend and girlfriend. We would arrive together for lunch in whichever room my aunt was keeping the food heated. Handkerchiefs would swag from the waistband of my brother's pants, to be plucked, besopped, then set free. I watched them sail toward the floor, each with a fresh fortune of phlegm.

"He always claimed his wife hated him for the wrong reasons," my aunt said. (I am afraid I paraphrase.) "Her despisal, he felt, was wide of the mark. The marriage was far from finished, but there was less to make it stick. The bed they shared was amiss. The mattress was too big for the frame, for one thing. There was quite the overhang on his side of it. He got better at shifting his weight onto other people, or tacking somebody onto himself for purposes of symmetry alone. I was much the same way—younger. But did I run? We were too much alike in our bloodbeat. We'd gone out to eat, finally, and he told me what he had told her exactly as he had put it to her: 'You, you, *you*.' Everywhere you look—why didn't I know it then?—people are repeating to other people what they had said to third parties, and the ones caught in the middle are afraid everyone within earshot will think that they, the middle people, are the ones being spoken to with such a tongue. So they keep interrupting. They say things like, 'You actually said that to so-and-so?' Emphasis on the so-and-so. But I hadn't been around long enough to know.

"My heart back then was more of a catch basin than it is now.

"When he was a child, mind you, he slept so soundly, he had to be taught everything all over again in the mornings—how to sit up to the table, what forks were for. His sisters were Brenna, Linette, and Naomi. They jumped for joy over whatever a foul little mouth could reach. He never wanted me to know their names and their interests. 'Disaggregate,' he'd say if he were here. He'd be throwing up his arms all over again.

"He would doff his shoes the instant he entered the house. 'You've no idea what I've been stepping in all day,' he'd say. He'd say farewell before shutting the door for his bath. I once found the poor man trying to read his way around a business card some thoughtless cuss had left as a bookmark midway down the page in a library book. I could see the struggle in him. The thing was slotted right into the spine, like a tiny extra page. It stuck out an angle. It was obvious he did not want to have to touch it. From where I stood, I could see the parallelogrammatic shadow it was throwing onto the left-hand page. I reached over and snatched it away. I was always the one to turn on the lamp and make sure the light fell over his left shoulder. I'd say, 'You'll ruin your eyes.' And he'd say, 'The only way to ruin your eyes is to keep looking at people.'

"So don't think I don't know what you two think you have," my aunt said. "Don't pretend you're the first."

I had my foot around my brother's ankle. One of his hands was in mine; the other grasped an undrabbled handkerchief.

"He knocked you up?" I said.

"It was during one of the later years upstairs," my aunt said. "The doctors told us it was a termless pregnancy, that the child might not ever come out, that it wasn't going anywhere, that you see these sorts of impactions every once in a very great while, that this wasn't the end of the world, there were ways to get around things, arrangements could be made for its tutoring, its recreations, inside of me, and for a while we kept at it, the drills, the columns of words, the recommended rhymes. But we started hearing less and less in return. 'Pipe up!' I would shout. It got harder to tell its baby talk, as muffled as it was, from everything else that might have been going on in my hellhole of a body proper. I think sooner or later it must have just got drowned out. I know I started shedding pounds."

"Do you ever talk to him?" I said.

"Your father?" my aunt said.

•

A couple of nights later, I heard heavy luggage landing on the linoleum below. We were all three of us on the floor. My head was in my brother's lap. I thought I was the only one awake.

"Who got the decorations out?" my father shouted from downstairs. "Who gave anyone permission to hang crepe paper?"

We lay still. I could see my aunt's eyes unclosing themselves.

"What did I miss?" my father shouted. "Something big? Somebody thinks they had another wedding behind my back? That's what this is about?"

I heard drawers being opened heatedly.

"What else could have happened?" my father shouted. "Look at this place."

I heard the oven door slam.

"Which one of you?" my father shouted.

I saw my aunt raise an arm from the elbow, then start to bring it down. I kicked out my leg and caught the arm before the fist could reach the wide, booming floor.

SIX STORIES

SIMPLE

This is the simplest story. Why am I always the one to tell it?

When I was nine, an older kid said, "Hold out your hand." Then tossed a crumpled candy-bar wrapper into my obediently cupped palm.

Walked away, laughing.

I decided to let the wrapper stay put.

Out of spite, or what?

I grew up, rented a room, worked, rode escalators, figured out where and where not to insert myself.

People kept looking at the wrapper in my hand and saying, "Here, let me take care of that for you," or "Are you looking for something?"

I kept waiting for somebody to say something in a language that wasn't shot.

CONCENTRATION

There was eventually a little something wrong with the son, too, though nothing so bad as with the daughter. The parents ordered corrective shoes and sat up late one night, writing and recopying and then laminating a note to be passed among all of his teachers.

The teachers read the note and placed the son at a special desk, where they quizzed him about kings and invertebrates. He answered bodily, and correctly.

He came home having been taught how to answer the telephone in a telephone voice.

"Speaking," he had been taught to say.

His one big break was being told he needed eyeglasses—an encumbering portable fenestration that made props of his nose and ears. It was not so much that the world was now filled in more tidily (things were less destitute of outline, less likely to drown within themselves before they arrived in the thick of his eye) as that he felt he had acquired a wicket about himself, a little cage up front through which business could get quickly and fittingly done.

I WAS SURER OF THINGS

Try it this way: there was a woman who betrayed me with a man who had opened a factory in which it was suggested that the workers make things out of glass. The man did not believe in pushing people. He never once looked over anyone's shoulder.

The man had no luck in hiring the woman's children.

They lived off their mother and grew demandingly lovely on two slipcovered sofas pushed together end to end.

Coarse, dandelionish tufts of fabric sewn at intervals into the slipcovers left pink imprints on their cheeks, their foreheads.

I later liked to watch them walking ably away from me but not yet toward each other.

I will not give you any of the gore.

EMPLOYMENT

I'm looking for work in this room, naturally. I'm desiring lots of work in this room. I'm very serious about my desire.

I go up to the guy. "Is there work?" I ask.

"I would imagine," he says. He shows me to the desk. It's the same old desk, my desk.

I pull out the chair and sit down.

I open one of the drawers. I find my underwear and socks exactly where I keep them. I open another and find my health-and-beauty aids.

The guy says, "You get dental, eyeglass, life insurance, major medical, death and dismemberment, two weeks' paid vacation, seven paid holidays, fifteen paid sick days, personal days TBA. Employee pilfering is the retail sector's filthiest of secrets. Lift with your whole body, not with your limbs. Don't just be a people person—be a person's person. Come in through the employees' entrance and breathe out through your nose. This concludes the orientation."

I reach for a pen.

He slaps my hand hard.

"Just do what you'd be doing anyway," he says. "Only now it's going to be work."

SPEAK UP

She wants to know what he saw in her, so I reach right in for it, pluck it out, and hand it to her. It's a grammatical occurrence of something big, something way out of scale.

This is a conversation we're having, an incident. She is hemming his trousers, the six pair he left behind. I have been encouraging her to wear them herself—one pair per day of the week, time off on Wednesday, middle of the week, in case she runs out of anecdotal material.

In short, I tell her, Hate him.

But she wants to know what if he calls, what if he comes back, what if they're both shopping for memo pads in the same micromart.

Skip it, I tell her.

To be fair, what goes where? In terms of my life, where should this be taking up places?

The only way this keeps going is if you speak up.

Tell me something.

Tell me every other thing.

How's every other thing?

THIS STORY

This story has two parts.

The first is about his last love—how he got circumstanced in it, and all the antiperspirants and behaving and abbreviations it later came to entail. This part is long—much too long for me to include or even synopsize here—and it darts out at this or that. Please do not hold it against me if I pretend that this part of the story was misplaced or, better, put aside to boil.

The second part of the story is short and familiar. It parallels your own life, so it is that much the easier to remember. It lends itself handily to discussion in groups small and still smaller. I will recite it in its entirety:

Son, you cunt!

LOO

Shall we face something else?

I had a sister once.

The center square of the little city where she had grown up still had a couple of "comfort stations." That was what they called those belowground public lavatories whose stairwelled entrances, sided and canopied with frosted glass, looked like gateways to some sunken Victorian exposition. She could not remember whether she simply wasn't allowed down there or just preferred holding it in.

This sister was the self-silencing type.

She was done up in a body bereft of freckles or shine.

She never found a way to get her hair rioting upward in the flaring fashion of her time.

Loo (for that was the name she used) was already at that stage in her headway toward demise where it was best to tell people what they wanted to hear. What they mostly wanted to hear was that nobody else, no matter her station in life, ever really knew how much it was she should by now have gone ahead and packed.

•

Her sleep in those days was generous to a fault. But she would wake up and feel herself felled by the clarities and definitudes of the new day. Then to work, in the afternoons, in a windowless basement office in an overchilled building on the outskirts of town. There would sometimes be too rational a cast to her mind, and sometimes she nodded off, but this was an ungiving, dream-free species of sleep and did not want her in it. There was nothing to be made of it, either. It left no residue.

•

She was a remainder of her parents, not a reminder of them.

Her private life was not so much private as simply witnessless.

The shops in those days did in fact sell something called a "body pillow," but she had not brought any of them home yet.

•

Her second job was an older person's job.

She was afraid there was nothing she didn't find entirely mysterious, nothing that didn't make her feel as if she had never once belonged in her life. But the two or three people to whom she had been closest had always been the most difficult to fathom or even unveil. Even their faces seemed to destabilize themselves into new forms of unrecognizability under the hardly forceful pressure of her gaze. She would no longer know who the person was that was morphing disorganizingly before her eyes while the two of them were eating or pretending not to be hungry or doing whatever they did that kept them together undefended. She would have no steadying sense of what the person truly looked like from one instant to the next. And if the externals were themselves so mutable, there could be no end to speculation about what exactly might be going on inside any human body purposely neighboring her own. There was no reliable way of finding out. Everything she claimed to understand about people was no more than hazarded.

She wanted to convince herself that there was a way to learn how she might securely know just one thing, maybe a couple of things, about any other person—if only the most persuasive of that person's reasons for having hated his handwriting at the moment it came time at last to make a list of things that must change absolutely right away or else.

•

Other things that brought a better grade of sorrow into her world, broadened her agony, etc.?

She had the disadvantage of apparently looking like a lot of other people, because she was often accosted by strangers who took it for granted that she was somebody they knew, and they insisted on resuming conversations broken off long ago and threw fits when she could not supply the precise lines of flattery or remorse they had been waiting all this long while to hear.

She had been living for some disorderly time in furnitureless, dun-colored small-town apartments with the blinds drawn at all hours. She had never learned the names of the streets. She had only a punctured knowledge of geography. She supposed that it helped her to be far from the center of anything, never incited by what went on in thicker populations.

•

Looking too long unfondled, she would doubtless have a different answer now, but coach herself forward she did. A heavy-haired girl of terrorizing ordinary beauty cornered her, unpeppily, at some upstairs cabaret, but were teems of feeling fizzing between the two of them afterward? Or did memory spoon out some garniture of emotion over everything taking its time in catty months to come?

Nothing nestled in her remembrance.

There were belongings to buy, and a ruesomeness incompressible into any of the words she knew, and a past already kaput and ready to rebulk, rebuke.

But twenty-two, twenty-three—she was running out of realms.

•

Or it was just that she had such an overacquaintance with herself, suffered from such an oppressive overintimacy with her body and the contents of her every minute, that on those rare occasions when she stumbled upon a glimpse of the bigger picture of herself, and actually got a look at the contours of her life, she was practically undone—because the microscopic view and the larger perspective did not fit together at all. So she was plunged into a disabling uncertainty that at length infected her speech and gave her trouble with the first-person pronouns, because the range of reference was now clouded and baffling.

•

There were jolts and didders to her nervous system.

Her life did not so much advance as narrow itself out unamelioratingly.

But did she shoplift?

With fingers so thin they looked like snippets from somebody else's?

•

She was not blessed with a voice in the head that furnished a running interpretation of human incident. Lives around her motioned brokenly this way and that. She made herself more available, visible, riskful. But even her own body would not honor her. There were flubs in her private locations, and her hands did not mix all that well with each other.

•

There was in fact less and less talk in her life, and when she did speak, it was as if the words were issuing not from her mouth but from some rent in the murk of her being. It was the penetralia speaking for once and at last. So what came out did not sound that much like ordinary utterancy but came crashing out of the vocabulary she kept crashing herself against.

Her bugginess and obsessions and sexual instabilities were probably never that far from home, though they were mostly a tiny and shrinking department of her life.

It was a life into which others now and again must have pitched some of their woe.

•

Our mother?

Two parties must be present at every birth.

Neither ever survives in one way or another.

•

While she was growing up, some packages of potato chips used to carry, on their backsides, a defensive notation along the lines of "This package is sold by weight, not by volume. Contents may have settled during shipment." It put her in mind of daily, unshapeful life—though the generalizings about it would carry her only farther and farther away from where she was trying to throw herself at the first perfectly rotten mood to come along in anyone looking more likely to last.

•

And our father?

As a girl, she must have known it was a coin collection, at least of sorts. But the nickels and silver dollars had not been pressed into any of those gloomy folders from some hobby shop.

My sister needed the chocolate teenies, the sourballs, the licoriced whatnots.

•

She was big on upshots and bitter ends, but she did not see herself as polarizing. Why should she have to see herself at all? That was somebody else's affliction, not hers. She had learned long ago how to prepare herself for a day without recourse to a mirror.

It was in the restrooms of cosmetology colleges, restaurants with communal tables, underemployment agencies, off-price stores, that her fingers offered herself and others a fugitive and unimproving satisfaction of a kind, though she otherwise lacked the reach that life was said to require.

•

She did not like to drive, she suffered motion sickness on trains, planes were much too aerial for her taste, and on buses she would get stuck next to the perspirational, the heartsore.

She was uncottoned-to, but a soft touch always.

•

She audited an Oral Communications class at the township college. But despite all that dreamy speech-course certitude about "messages" and their "senders" and awaiting "receivers" (those textbook diagrams with the perkily curving arrows always made her sad), wasn't most communication of any sort a one-way street anyway? Shouldn't she have been content with the inner sentences of hers going on for miles and miles—an entire continent's worth, for that matter—without anyone in any oncoming traffic taking any notice whatsoever?

The professor said things like "Other things being equal" and backed drably away from her after class. He looked cramped and made sport of in his own life and forums. There was a turnout of papules, ingrown hairs, whiteheads, on his face. Her final grade was a Courier-font C.

•

Of the flight home for the first of the funerals, she remembered little except that the couple sitting to her left kept rousing her from her narcosis (she had chewn some stupefacients) so they could use the restroom. They always left and returned as a couple.

She hoped she hadn't been talking in her sleep. A big fear was that in her sleep she would "open up" and give untidy, exploded views of her psyche.

•

Later still: that dick-ridden gleam to her, the razzmatazz of her makeup, an autumn with a winterly girl (lavish of eyeliner and with that knack for the pathetical), then newer and newer dips to her sadness, and the panache of her about-faces to follow: setting foot out of herself, or making overtures to herself—she owed it to herself to see life flatten itself desirably in the very design of a day.

•

Then where—Kansas, Arkansas? The paychecks were direct-deposited, so you tended to forget.

She felt cozy in the time zone, but her days out there were as livelong as all get-out.

In those parts, the supermarket bakeries baked bagels without even a hole.

There was a diary for a while. She dressed page after page in a sneaky, tossing backhand:

Rubbing: I came to it late and didn't get a whole lot out of it. My life, so help me, has been little more than an ongoing demonstration of the fiasco of the bodily.

Other pages, I later saw, concerned the ruck and malarkey of monthly life, the unwondersome ways in which people finished with each other.

•

I like to think she might have said something quieteningly final and fair enough.

I bought a car, a black one, and drove it. I let the thing fill up with more and more trash.

In next to no time, the driver's side had been keyed intricately, all-overishly, though perhaps *keyed* is not quite the word. There must have been ice picks and chisels involved as well.

PARTIAL LIST OF PEOPLE TO BLEACH

She was either next to me on a plane and turning a page of her magazine every time I turned one of mine, or else she had come forward from way back to be a handful anew, because people repeat on you or otherwise go unplundered. I will think of her as Aisler for any priggish intentions I might still manage here.

Aisler had spousy eyes, and arms exemplary in their plunges, and she brought her bare knees together until they were buttocky and practical. I hemmed and hawed inside of her for some weeks after but never got the hang of her requirements. A woman that swaggering of heart will not bask in deferred venereal folderol.

Anyway, she had a kid, and the kid's questions kept tripping me up—e.g., if you let people walk all over you, do you become a *place?*

Seven, seven and a half, and there were tiny whelms of hair already all over the guy.

I was flushy, heavy-faced, bluntly forty.

The morning they moved out (this was winter; flurries quibbled at the window), I made a sinking study of the lease. I had never given much thought to its terms before, the deductional verve of "lessor," "lessee." I was worded into the thing just once as an accountable, but the woman's name was right and left, gothicked in fountain-pen flaunts.

In short, I left the apartment the way I had found it—evacuated, fakedly intact, incapacitated for any glorying course of residential circumstance.

This was the demising district's lone block of limestone heights.

I had lived there wreckingly in pairs, and in notional associations of greater than two. I had painted many a rosy picture. My eyes, it had usually been claimed, were bigger than my asshole.

So I stored some things, some becalming ensembles, in my car of the decade, a four-door sobriety. Set out for a pay phone, called some people to ask after people even sparser. But after a while it was just their biles vying with mine.

•

Night was a portal to the morning, maybe, but morning was no gateway.

At the office campus: a couple of new hires on my level, a woman and a man. The man was in his meridian twenties, not a quick one to color. It was all I could do to show him the quickest way to disable a paper clip so it could no longer get a purchase on the pages; how to refuse food from people who came in one day with new teeth shingled over the old.

There were spatter-dash cookies all week the week he started.

We had, this new one and I, some jaunty pleasance in the john. We carried on without bywords or backwash, got to the bottom of our camaraderie pronto. He was inconclusively beautiful, a crude breather through it all, and I was easy to glut, even easier to usher out.

The other new one, the woman, gleamed in her attendance. She was one of those life-leading types newly mired. Her hair looked created just for the day.

•

A daughter of hers came in one morning, came over to my desk, uncautioned. She was jeweled meanly and sloping well out of her twenties, and said, "I do sense a life boarded up inside you."

She let a hand deaden decently on my knee.

I made an appointment to meet her at the close of the week outside some vocational library beyond the county.

The day came (and so soon!) with a new droop to the sky. I drove out to the place, parked, welcomed a wait. She showed, though with a readied but refraining woman of her own. Just a girl with blacked-up, secluding hair, attractively uncertain in a man's raincoat, a fraternal-looking thing.

I went off with the second.

Her apartment, a duplex—lawn chairs everywhere inside, an unheightened futon local to the dining room, track lamps watted lowly. It was a vague body she had, the breasts just glib, simple growths. The mossy hair on her wrists—lichen, rather, it looked like—took a weak but exact tack down her back, too. I was grateful for the broadway of bone that ran the wan length of it.

The usual skewing of selves, and then a brother upstairs if I felt I needed a look.

I did later make it up the steps. Found him adrowse undrunkenly in the tub. (The water hued, perfumed, kept bubblish with pumps. Wind chimes strung from the showerhead and set chinkling by an electric fan.)

Above the waterline: the snuggery of his underarms, an unhardihood to the shoulder blades—the healing neck, the face sharp-featured and finagledly beardless.

He talked; said he hoped to be seen as a behaving presence thereafter. Said he wanted to look traveled and dressy from a distance. Saw himself as an original in strickenness, long uncopied.

I took a seat on the toilet.

Did I agree, in maybe theory, that there were the taken, and the takers, and, between them, the kinds catastrophizing quietly?

A hand came suffering upward from the suds.

Tell the truth, he said: didn't I now feel *teamed?*

I sat some more, then felt fickle, went back downstairs to sit a while longer with the sister. But the arms I put around people always met up again with each other.

•

It was fitting to call our sessions at our desks "shifts," because shift I did—I mean, I fended, scraped along, moved from one point to a point just beyond. There was a lunchroom where I referred crackers backhandedly into my mouth, and a lobby with a guard who stood with hirsute goodwill behind a counter, and a restroom off the lobby. Above the urinals: a "PLEASE FLUSH" sign, with a clip-art elephant and "Don't Forget!" scripted down its trunk. But I wanted my piss pooling, maturing, in the bowl with everybody else's.

The day widened as you tired of it.

This still was Thursday. Then Friday finally underfoot. Then a three-day weekend, a second-string holiday thought necessary to observe.

I knew enough to go home. The route was more formal now, with toll-takers trained to thank. Then an oncoming car not far from the turnoff, and I slipped up—got the windshield wipers going by mistake.

I was afraid the swipes might be taken for communication or, worse yet, a wave.

Then a pyloned bridge, the spotless boulevards, thinning streets of close-set addresses.

My folks! They had each overshot their marriage but otherwise went about ungulfed by life. They welcomed me back to their shams. Nothing was amiss or cosmic in my old, dormered room upstairs. A promising first gush of sleep, and then I awoke to the usual voices pluming upward through the baseboards.

I had not got a whole lot out of my heritage except a hoarseness like his, a poked heart on the order of her own.

They were savvier in their lamentations now.

•

Forty I was, and then fortier, fluking through my annual reviews, carrying my deskside trash home at the end of a day rather than running any risk of its being examined.

Just an inkling of skyline to this city. Nobody had thought to get lyrical about it yet. I was living on the brink of downtown but not, so to speak, alone.

There was an injuring party in his tindery fifties, and another, only lately unbunched from a family, querying out of some hole.

Then one who may have gone on to ape something wonderful.

And yet another, much younger: wronged early on, then doctored, restarted, struck by blows again. She had eyes of a deep, speaking green, but it was a green that spoke differently in a day's time.

I could roll off the names, the work numbers, of them all.

I could let a little thing or two ruin every other thing.

Things true of me should be even truer of you.

Sometimes people are too close to call.

THE SENTENCE IS
A LONELY PLACE

I came to language only late and only peculiarly. I grew up in
a household where the only books were the telephone book
and some coloring books. Magazines, though, were called
books, but only one magazine ever came into the house:
a now-long-gone photographic general-interest weekly
commandingly named *Look*. Words in this household were
not often brought into play. There were no discussions that
I can remember, no occasions when language was called
for at length or in bulk. Words seemed to be intruders,
blown into the rooms from otherwhere through the
speakers of the television set or the radio, and were easily
ignorable as something alien, something not germane to
the forlornities of life within the house, and readily shut off
or shut out. Under our roof, there was more divulgence and
expressiveness to be made out in the closing or opening of
doors, in footfalls, in coughs and stomach growlings and
other bodily ballyhoo, than in statements exchanged in
occasional conversation. Words seemed to be a last resort:
you had recourse to speech only if everything else failed.
From early on, it seemed to me that the forming and the
release of words were the least significant of the mouth's
activities. When words did come hazarding out of a mouth,
they did not lastingly change anything about the mouth

they were coming out of or the face that hosted the mouth. They often seemed to have been put in there by some force exterior to the person speaking, and they died out in the air. They were not something I could possess or store up. Words certainly weren't inside me.

A word that I remember coming out of my parents' mouths a lot was *imagine*—as in "I imagine we're going to have rain." I soon succumbed to the notion that to imagine was to claim to know in advance an entirely forgettable outcome. A calendar was hung in the kitchen as if to say: Expect more of the same.

I thus spent about the first thirteen or fourteen years of my life not having much of anything to do with language. I am told that once in a while I spoke up. I am told that I had a friend at some point, and this friend often corrected my pronunciations, which tended to be overliteral, and deviant in their distribution of stresses. Any word I spoke, often as not, sounded like two words of similar length that had crashed into each other. Word after word emerged from my mouth as a mumbled mongrel. I was often asked to repeat things, and the repeated version came forth as a skeptical variant of the first one and was usually offered at a much lower volume. When a preposition was called for in a statement, I often chose an unfitting one. If a classmate asked me, "When is band practice?," I would be likely to answer, "At fifth period." I did not have many listeners, and I did not listen to myself. Things I spoke came out sounding instantly disowned.

Childhood in my generation, an unpivotal generation, wasn't necessarily a witnessed phenomenon. Large portions of my day went unobserved by anyone else, even in classrooms. Anybody glimpsing me for an instant might have described me as a kid with his nose stuck in a book, but nobody would have noticed that I wasn't reading. I had started to gravitate toward books only because a book was a kind of steadying accessory, a prop, something to grip—a simple occupation for my hands. (Much later, I was relieved to learn that librarians refer to the books and other printed matter in their collections as "holdings.") And at some point I started to enjoy having a book open before me and beholding the comfortingly justified lineups and amassments of words. I liked seeing words on parade on the pages, but I never got in step with them, I never entered into the processions. I doubt that it often even occurred to me to read the books, although I know I knew how. Instead, I liked how anything small (a pretzel crumb, perhaps) that fell into the gutter of the book—that troughlike place where facing pages meet—stayed in there and was preserved. A book was, for me, an acquisitive thing, absorbing, accepting, taking into itself whatever was dropped into it. An opened book even seemed to me an invitation to practice hygiene over it—to peel off the rim of a fingernail, say, and let the thing find its way down onto a page. The book became a repository of the body's off-trickles, extrusions, biological rubbish and remains; it became a reliquary of sorts. I was thuswise now archiving chance fragments, sometimes choice fragments, of my life. I was putting things into the books instead of withdrawing their offered contents. As usual, I had things backward.

Worse, the reading we were doing in school was almost always reading done sleepily aloud, our lessons consisting of listening to the chapters of a textbook, my classmates and I taking our compulsory turns at droning through a double-columned page or two; and I, for one, never paid much mind to what was being read. The words on the page seemed to have little utility other than as mere prompts or often misleading cues for the sluggard sounds we were expected to produce. The words on the page did not seem to have solid enough a presence to exist independently of the sounds. I had no sense that a book read in silence and in private could offer me something. I can't remember reading anything with much comprehension until eighth grade, when, studying for a science test for once, I decided to try making my way quietly through the chapter from start to finish—it was a chapter about magnets—and found myself forced to form the sounds of the words in my head as I read.

Many of the words were unfamiliar to me, but the words fizzed and popped and tinkled and bonged. I was reading so slowly that in many a word I heard the scrunch and flump of the consonants and the peal of the vowels. Granted, I wasn't retaining much of anything, but almost every word now struck me as a provocative hullabaloo. This was my first real lesson about language—this inkling that a word is a solid, something firm and palpable. It was news to me that a word is matter, that it exists in tactual materiality, that it has a cubic bulk. Only on the page is it flat and undensified. In the mouth and in the mind it is three-dimensional, and there are parts that shoot out from it or sink into its syntactic surround. But this discovery was of no help to me in English class, because when we had to write, I could never call up any of the brassy and racketing words I had read, and fell back on the thin, flat, default vocabulary of my life at home, words spoken because no others were known or available. Even when I started reading vocabulary-improvement books, I never seemed capable of importing into my sentences any of the vivid specimens from the lists I had now begun to memorize. My writing was dividered from the arrayed opulences in the vocabulary books. Language remained beyond me. My distance from language continued even through college, even through graduate school. The words I loved were in a different part of me, not accessible to the part of me that was required to make statements on paper.

It took me almost another decade after graduate school to figure out what writing really is, or at least what it could be for me; and what prompted this second lesson in language was my discovery of certain remaindered books—mostly of fiction, most notably by Barry Hannah, and all of them, I later learned, edited by Gordon Lish—in which virtually every sentence had the force and feel of a climax, in which almost every sentence was a vivid extremity of language, an abruption, a definitive inquietude. These were books written by writers who recognized the sentence as the one true theater of endeavor, as the place where writing comes to a point and attains its ultimacy. As a reader, I finally knew what I wanted to read, and as someone now yearning to become a writer, I knew exactly what I wanted to try to write: narratives of steep verbal topography, narratives in which the sentence is a complete, portable solitude, a minute immediacy of consummated language—the sort of sentence that, even when liberated from its receiving context, impresses itself upon the eye and the ear as a totality, an omnitude, unto itself. I once later tried to define this kind of sentence as "an outcry combining the acoustical elegance of the aphorism with the force and utility of the load-bearing, tractional sentence of more or less conventional narrative." The writers of such sentences became the writers I read and reread. I favored books that you could open to any page and find in every paragraph sentences that had been worked and reworked until their forms and contours and their organizations of sound had about them an air of having been foreordained—as if this combination of words could not be improved upon and had finished readying itself for infinity.

And as I encountered any such sentence, the question I would ask myself in marvelment was: how did this thing come to be what it now is? This was when I started gazing into sentence after sentence and began to discover that there was nothing arbitrary or unwitting or fluky about the shape any sentence had taken and the sound it was releasing into the world.

I'll try to explain what it is that such sentences all seem to have in common and how in fact they might well have been written.

•

The sentence, within its narrow typographical confines, is a lonely place, the loneliest place for a writer, and the temptation for the writer to get out of one sentence as soon as possible and get going on the next sentence is entirely understandable. In fact, the conditions in just about any sentence soon enough become (shall we admit it?) claustrophobic, inhospitable, even hellish. But too often our habitual and hasty breaking away from one sentence to another results in sentences that remain undeveloped parcels of literary real estate, sentences that do not feel fully inhabited and settled in by language. So many of the sentences we confront in books and magazines look unfinished and provisional, and start to go to pieces as soon as we gawk at and stare into them. They don't hold up. Their diction is often not just spare and stark but bare and miserly.

There is another way to look at this:

The sentence is the site of your enterprise with words, the locale where language either comes to a head or does not. The sentence is a situation of words in the most literal sense: words must be situated in relation to others to produce an enduring effect on a reader. As you situate the words, you are of course intent on obeying the ordinances of syntax and grammar, unless any willful violation is your purpose—and you are intent as well on achieving in the arrangements of words as much fidelity as is possible to whatever you believe you have wanted to say or describe. A lot of writers—too many of them—unfortunately seem to stop there. They seem content if the resultant sentence is free from obvious faults and is faithful to the lineaments of the thought or feeling or whatnot that was awaiting deathless expression. But some other writers seem to know that it takes more than that for a sentence to cohere and flourish as a work of art. They seem to know that the words inside the sentence must behave as if they were destined to belong together—as if their separation from each other would deprive the parent story or novel, as well as the readerly world, of something life-bearing and essential. These writers recognize that there needs to be an intimacy between the words, a togetherness that has nothing to do with grammar or syntax but instead has to do with the very shapes and sounds, the forms and contours, of the gathered words. This intimacy is what we mean when we say of a piece of writing that it has a felicity—a fitness, an aptness, a rightness about the phrasing. The words in the sentence must bear some physical and sonic resemblance to each other—the way people and their dogs are said to come to resemble each other, the way children take after their parents, the way pairs and groups of friends evolve their own manner of dress and gesture and speech. A pausing, enraptured reader should be able to look deeply into the sentence and discern among the words all of the traits and characteristics they share. The impression to be given is that the words in the sentence have lived with each other for quite some time, *decisive* time, and have deepened and grown and matured in each other's company—and that they cannot live without each other.

Here is what I believe seems to happen in such a sentence:

Once the words begin to settle into their circumstance in a sentence and decide to make the most of their predicament, they look around and take notice of their neighbors. They seek out affinities, they adapt to each other, they begin to make adjustments in their appearance to try to blend in with each other better and enhance any resemblance. Pretty soon in the writer's eyes the words in the sentence are all vibrating and destabilizing themselves: no longer solid and immutable, they start to flutter this way and that in playful receptivity, taking into themselves parts of neighboring words, or shedding parts of themselves into the gutter of the page or screen; and in this process of intimate mutation and transformation, the words swap alphabetary vitals and viscera, tiny bits and dabs of their languagey inner and outer natures; the words intermingle and blend and smear and recompose themselves. They begin to take on a similar typographical physique. The phrasing now feels literally all of a piece. The lonely space of the sentence feels colonized. There's a sumptuousness, a roundedness, a dimensionality to what has emerged. The sentence feels filled in from end to end; there are no makeshift segments along its length, no pockets of unperforming or underperforming verbal matter. The words of the sentence have in fact formed a united community.

Or, rather, if the words don't manage to do this all by themselves—because maybe they mostly won't— you will have to nudge them along in the process. You might come to realize that a single vowel already present in the sentence should be released to run through the consonantal frameworks of certain other prominent words in the sentence, or you might realize that the consonantal infrastructure of one word should be duplicated in another word, but with a different vowel impounded in each structure. You might wonder what would become of a word at one end of a sentence if an affix were thrust upon it from a word at the other end, or what might happen if the syntactical function of a word were shifted from its present part of speech to some other. And as the words reconstitute themselves and metamorphose, your sentence may begin to make a series of departures from what you may have intended to express; the language may start taking on, as they say, a life of its own, a life that contests or trumps the life you had sponsored to live on the page. But it was you who incited these words to shimmer and mutate and reconfigure even further—and what they now are saying may well be much more acute and more crucial than what you had thought you wanted to say.

I think this is the only way to explain what happens to my own sentences during those very rare occasions when I am writing the way I want to write, and it seems to account for how sentences by writers I admire have arisen from the alphabet. The aim of the literary artist, I believe, is to initiate the process by which the words in a sentence no longer remain strangers to each other but begin to acknowledge one another's existence and do more than tolerate each other's presence in the phrasing: the words have to lean on each other, rub elbows, rub off on each other, feel each other up. Among contemporary writers of fiction, there are few who have reliably achieved what I am calling an intra-sentence intimacy with more exquisiteness and grace than Christine Schutt, especially in her first novels *Florida* and *Prosperous Friends* and in her second collection of short stories, *A Day, a Night, Another Day, Summer.*

Let's first look inside only a four-word phrase of hers.

In her story "The Blood Jet," Schutt ends a sentence about "life after a certain age" by describing it capsularly as "acutely felt, clearly flat"—two pairs of words in which an adverb precedes an adjective. The adjectives (*felt* and *flat*) are both monosyllabic, they are both four letters in length, and they both share the same consonantal casing: they begin with a tentative-sounding, deflating *f* and end with the abrupt *t*. In between the two ends of each adjective, Schutt retains the *l*, though it slides one space backward in the second adjective; and for the interior vowel, she moves downward from a short *e* to a short *a*. The predecessive adverbs *acutely* and *clearly* share the *k*-sounding *c*, and both words are constituted of virtually the same letters, except that *clearly* doesn't retain the *t* of *acutely*. The four-word phrase has a resigned and final sound to it; there is more than a little agony in how, with just two little adjustments, *felt* has been diminished and transmogrified into *flat*, in how the richness of receptivity summed up in *felt* has been leveled into the thudding spiritlessness of *flat*. All of this emotion has been delivered by the most ordinary of words—nothing dredged up from a thesaurus. But what is perhaps most striking about the four-word phrase is the family resemblances between the two pairs of words. There is nothing in the letter-by-letter makeup of the phrase "clearly flat" that isn't already physically present in "acutely felt"; the second of the two phrases contains the alphabetic DNA of the first phrase. There isn't, of course, an exact, anagrammatic correspondence between the two pairs of words; the *u* of the first pair, after all, hasn't been carried over into the second pair. (Schutt isn't stooping to recreational word games.) But the page-hugging, rather than page-turning, reader—the very reader whom a writer such as Schutt enthralls—cannot help noticing that the second phrase is a selective rearrangement, a selective redisposition, of the first one—a declension, really, as if, within the verbal environment of the story, there were no other direction for the letters in the first pair of words to go. There is nothing random about what has happened here. Schutt's phrase has achieved the condition that Susan Sontag, in her essay about the prose of poets, called "lexical inevitability."

Before we turn our eyes and ears to the entirety of a two-clause structure by Christine Schutt, maybe we can agree that almost every word in a sentence can be categorized as either a content word or a functional word. The content words comprise the nouns, the adjectives, the adverbs, and most verbs: they are carriers of information and suppliers of sensory evidence. The functional words are the prepositions, the conjunctions, the articles, the *to* of an infinitive, and such—the kinds of words necessary to hold the content words in place on the page, to absorb them into the syntax. The functional words in fact tend to recede into the sentence structure; their visibility and audibility are limited. It's the content words that impress themselves upon the eye and the ear, so the writer's attention to sound and shape has to be lavished on the exposed words. They stand out in relief. (Pronouns, of course, do not quite fit tidily into this binary system; pronouns are prominent when appearing as subjects or objects but tend to shrink when serving in a possessive capacity. And some common verbs—especially those formed from the infinitives *to be* and *to have*—tend toward the unnoticeability of operational words.)

In Christine Schutt's two-clause formation "her lips stuck when she licked them to talk," the second half of a sentence from the short story "Young," the conspicuous content words are *lips*, *stuck*, *licked*, and *talk*. These four words are not all that varied consonantically. The reappearing consonants are *l* and *k*. Three of the four words have an *l*: two have the *l* at the very start of the word (*lips* and *licked*), and in the final word (*talk*), the *l* has slid into the interior. Three of the four words have a *k* in common—we go from a terminal *k* (*stuck*) to a *k* that has worked its way backward into the very core (*licked*) and then again to a terminal *k* (*talk*). In the first three words, the *l* and the *k* keep their distance from each other: in the first two words, they don't appear together; inside the third word, *licked*, they are now within kiss-blowing range of each other over the low-rising *i* and *c* that stand between them. In the final word, *talk*, the *l* and the *k* are side by side at last—coupled just before the period brings the curtain down. A romance between two letters has been enacted in the sentence: there has been an amorous progression toward union.

This kind of flirtation between two letters and their eventual matrimony brighten Christine Schutt's work not only in the individual sentence but in the paragraph as well. In the four-sentence opening paragraph of the story "The Summer after Barbara Claffey," in Schutt's first short-story collection, *Nightwork*, the characters *k* and *w* spend the first three sentences dancing around each other and sometimes tentatively touching, but their intimacy never gets more serious than the conventional embrace they entertain in the familiar participle *walking*:

> I once saw a man hook a walking stick around a woman's neck. This was at night, from my mother's window. The man dropped the crooked end behind the woman's neck and yanked just hard enough to get the woman walking to the car.

Letters, of course, are also known as characters, and it's a courtship between characters that creates an excitement in these sentences. The *w* seems warily feminine; the *k* seems brashly masculine. In the fourth and final sentence of the paragraph, the two characters mate and marry in the unexpected but beautifully apposite participle *winking*, a union resulting in what is in many ways the most stylistically noteworthy word in the paragraph. Then the *w* and the *k* disappear completely from what is left of the sentence as it plays itself out in a fade-out sequence of prepositional phrases:

> I saw this and saw rain winking in the yard in the light around our house.

Writing is rich to the extent that the drama of the subject matter is supplemented or deepened by the drama of the letters within the words as they inch their way closer to each other or push significantly off.

•

Gordon Lish—the enormously influential editor, writer, and teacher whom I mentioned earlier—instructed his students in a poetics of the sentence that emphasized what he called consecution: a recursive procedure by which one word pursues itself into its successor by discharging something from deep within itself into what follows. The discharge can take many forms and often produces startling outcomes, such as when Christine Schutt, in "The Summer after Barbara Claffey," is seeking the inevitable adjective to insert into the final slot in the sentence "Here is the house at night, lit up tall and _____." What she winds up doing is literally dragging forward the previous adjective, *tall*, and using it as the base on which further letters can be erected (while remaining mindful, as well, of the plaintive *ow* sound in the one concrete noun of the independent clause: *house*). The result is the astounding, perfect *tallowy*—the sort of adjective she never could have arrived at if she had turned a synonymicon upside down in search of words that capture the quality of light.

Gordon Lish's poetics forever changed the way I look at sentences, and so many of the sentences that thrill me are sentences in which consecution and recursion have determined the sound and the shape of the community of words. Take the aphoristic sentence that closes Diane Williams's story "Scratching the Head," in her second collection, *Some Sexual Success Stories Plus Other Stories in Which God Might Choose to Appear*: "An accident isn't necessarily ever over." There is so much to remark upon in this six-word, fifteen-syllable declaration. A sibilance hisses throughout *accident*, *isn't*, and *necessarily*; and in those three words there are further acoustical continuities—the *ih* sound moving forward from *accident* and into *isn't*, the *en* sound moving forward from *accident* and into *isn't* and into *necessarily*. In the five-syllable adverb *necessarily*, the vowel-and-consonant pair *ar* of the third syllable receives the primary stress, and the *ne* of the first syllable receives the secondary stress; and the *e* and the *r* of those two syllables get fillipped forward into *ever*, and then the dying fall of that adverb is echoed dyingly by *over*. *Ever* has morphed into *over*, of course, with nothing more than the substitution of an *o* for an *e*. These tumbly final words tumble out into a long vowel, the only long vowel of the sentence: the woe-laden, bemoaning long *o*. The final syllable of the sentence is unstressed, and this unaccentedness deprives the sentence of a hard, clean-cut termination, much as the import of the sentence insists that an accident lacks definitive finality.

A sentence that I have spent an almost pathological amount of time gaping at since the turn of the century, a sentence that always leaves me agog, is the opening sentence in Sam Lipsyte's story "I'm Slavering," in *Venus Drive*: "Everybody wanted everything to be gleaming again, or maybe they just wanted their evening back." The paraphrasal content of the statement informs us that high hopes for a return to a previous wealth of life or feeling are inevitably going to have to be scaled back and revised immediately and unconsolingly downward. If you tweak the verb tense from the past to the present, the sentence is even more self-containedly epigrammatic in its encompassing of our shared predicament of disappointments. It's a richly *summational* sentence, not the sort of sentence you might expect to find at the very outset of a story—but there are writers whose mission is sometimes to deliver us from conclusion to conclusion instead of necessarily bogging us down in the facts, the data, the sorry particulars leading to each conclusion.

Lipsyte's sentence is composed of words that, in ordinary hands, are among the most humdrum and pedestrian in our language: in the first half of the sentence alone, the words filling the subject slots in the independent clause and in the infinitive clause are the bland, heavily used indefinite pronouns *everybody* and *everything*. And the entire sentence is in fact completely lacking in specificity and so-called literary or elevated language: there is no load of detail, no verbal knickknackery whatsoever—there are no big-ticket words. The only standout word, the participle *gleaming*, most likely was called up into the sentence out of bits and pieces of the words preceding it—the ruling vowel of the entire utterance (the long *e*) and the *-ing* of *everything*. Yet this opening flourish of the story not only has both sweep and circumference in its stated meaning, but it has a swing and a lilt to it as well. The first half of the sentence is buoyant, upfloating. The entire sentence has the chiming, soaring, C-chord long *e*'s in *everybody* and *be* and *gleaming* and *maybe* and *evening*; it has the alliterative ballast of the *b*'s in *everybody* and *be* and *maybe* and *back*, and of the *g*'s in *gleaming* and *again*; and the only really *closed* word in the mix is the final word, the adverb *back*, which is shut off with harsh consonants at either end, especially the cruelly abrupt, terminal *k*, which finishes off the sentence and pushes it rudely down to earth. The last vowel in the sentence is the minor-key short *a* in *back*—the only appearance in the sentence of the disappointed, dejected *ahhh* of *crap* and *alas*.

•

Some of the most obvious ways to ensure that the words in a sentence together create a community of sound and shape are too rarely discussed explicitly outside of, say, high-school creative-writing classes. Yet many great writers constantly avail themselves of these little tactics to give their phrasing both dash and finish. The result is often a sentence that looks and sounds fulfilled, *permanent*. These phrasal maneuvers are concertedly evident in the examples I cited earlier, but they are worth considering individually, because even though we are all well acquainted with every one of them, we too easily forget just how much they can do for us.

For starters, make sure that the stressed syllables in a sentence outnumber the unstressed syllables. The fewer unstressed syllables there are, the more sonic impact the sentence will have, as in Don DeLillo's sentence "He did not direct a remark that was hard and sharp." You can take this stratagem to breath-stopping extremes, as Christine Schutt does in her sentence "None of what kept time once works." Schutt's sentence should remind us as well that we need not shy away from composing an occasional sentence entirely of monosyllabic words, as Barry Hannah also does in "I roam in the past for my best mind" and "He's been long on my list of shits in the world," and as Ben Marcus does in "They were hot there, and cold there, and some had been born there, and most had died."

Those sentences illustrate another point: unless you have good reason not to do so, end your sentence with the wham and bang of a stressed syllable, as in Dawn Raffel's sentence "She lived to marry late" and in John Ashbery's "There was I: a stinking adult." Such sentences stop on a dime instead of wavering forward for a wishy-washy further syllable or two.

At the opposite extreme, give force to your sentences by stationing the subject at the very beginning instead of delaying the subject until an introductory phrase or a dependent clause has first had its dribbling say. This precept of course violates almost every English-composition teacher's insistence that students vary the openings of their sentences, but you will find the best writers disobeying it as well. Readers have often attempted to account for the extraordinary cumulative power in the work of Joseph Mitchell, who wrote literary journalism for the *New Yorker* in a deceptively plain and simple style that often achieved incantatory cadences. You can make your way through pages and pages of Mitchell's gravely beautiful prose and almost never find him starting a sentence without laying down his subject at the outset. Many fiction writers also skip the preambles, as Dawn Raffel does in her sentence "She was born in December in Baraboo or thereabouts—small, still, blue, a girl, and, by some trick of oxygen, alive."

That Dawn Raffel sentence, with its recurring *b*'s and *l*'s, illustrates another form of play available to any writer. Avail yourself of alliteration—as long as it remains ungimmicky, unobtrusive, even subliminal. Such repetition can be soothing and stabilizing, especially in a sentence whose content and emotional gusts are anything but. You can let a single consonant dominate all or most of a sentence—the way Don DeLillo does with *h*'s in "He was here in the howl of the world," and as Christine Schutt does with *k* sounds in "He knew the kind of Kleenex crud a crying girl left behind." And the reiterated consonants do not have to appear at the beginnings of words: they can also show up at the very ends, as the *t*'s do in Barry Hannah's sentence "Ah, well, what you cannot correct you can at least insult," or they can be confined to the interiors of words, as the *l*'s are in Elizabeth Hardwick's sentence "Another day she arrived as wild and florid and thickly brilliant as a bird."

Take advantage of assonance as well. Keeping a single vowel in circulation through most of the conspicuous words will give a sentence another kind of sonic consummation, as Don DeLillo achieves with the five short *a*'s in "He mastered the steepest matters in half an afternoon," and as Sam Lipsyte does with three short *u*'s in "You could touch for a couple of bucks." (A lesser writer would of course have been satisfied with "For just two dollars, you could cop a feel.") Or reserve the assonance for the words in a sentence deserving the greatest stress, as Ben Marcus does in "The ones that never got born were poured into the river." You can even divide a sentence into two or more acoustical zones and let a single vowel prevail in each zone. Here is a three-zone sentence by Don DeLillo: "There were evening streaks in the white of the eye, a sense of blood sun."

You can make the most of both assonance and alliteration in a single sentence or multi-sentence sequence. In the following two-sentence run, Sam Lipsyte assonates with the long *oo* sound and alliterates with *p*'s and *k* sounds: "Dinner that night was some lewd stew I'd watched Parish concoct, undercooked carrots and pulled pork in ooze. I believe he threw some kiwi in there, too." Some writers take merged assonance and alliteration beyond slant rhymes or half rhymes (such as *lewd*, *stew*, and *ooze* in Lipsyte's first sentence) and even as far as a careful, unsingsongy kind of internal perfect rhyming, in which the rhyming words end with an identical vowel-and-consonant structure, as Fiona Maazel does in this sentence, which is acoustically unified further by the repeated *k* sounds: "I could tell she had been crying from the swell of her pores and the spackle crusted at the levees of each eye." And here are three samplings from the saddeningly neglected writer Elizabeth Smart, all from her short-fiction collection, *The Assumption of the Rogues & Rascals*: "This cliff, I thought, this office block, would certainly suit a suicide"; "The long fall is appalling"; and the aphoristically molded, five-word formulation "God likes a good frolic." In the last of these three sentences, there are all sorts of family resemblances among the words: the identical consonantic shells of *God* and *good* (as well as of *like* and the second syllable in *frolic*) and the shared vowel of *God* and *frolic*. And the way the words have been arrayed gives the sentence its aphoristic permanence. The article *a*, at the center of the statement, separates two phrases very similar in shape, with the words in the second phrase, *good frolic*, appearing as enlargements of, and elaborations on, the words in the first pair: *God likes*.

There are still further opportunities for you to work the uncanny into your phrasing. Press one part of speech into service as another, as Don DeLillo does in "She was always maybeing" (an adverb has been recruited for duty as a verb) and as Barry Hannah does in "Westy is colding off like the planet" (an adjective has been enlisted for verbified purpose as well). A variation is to take an intransitive verb (the sort of verb that can't abide a direct object) and put it in motion as a transitive verb (whose very nature it is to enclasp a direct object). That is what Fiona Maazel is up to with the verb *collide*, which abandoned all transitive use ages ago, in her sentence "Often, at the close of a recovery meeting, as we make a circle and join hands, I'll note the odds of these people finding each other in this group; our sundry pasts and principles; the entropy that collides addicts like so many molecules." Or take some standard, overworked idiomatic phrasing—such as "It turned my stomach"—and transfigure it, as Barry Hannah does in "I saw the hospital in Hawaii. It turned my heart." Or rescue an ordinary, overtasked verb from its usual drab business and find a fresh, bright, and startling context for it, as Don DeLillo manages with *speaks* in "You will hit traffic that speaks in quarter inches" and as Barry Hannah does with the almost always lackluster verb *occurred* in "… a single white wild blossom occurred under the forever stunted fig tree.…" You can also choose to prefer the unexpectable noun, as Diane Williams does with *history* in "We can come in out from our history to lie down" and as Sam Lipsyte does with *squeaks* in "Home, we drank a little wine, put on some of that sticky saxophone music we used to keep around to drown out the bitter squeaks in our hearts." Or you can choose a variant of a common word, a variant that exists officially in unabridged dictionaries but has fallen out of usage—if, that is, you have reason enough for doing so. In Fiona Maazel's sentence "This was not how I had meant to act, all tough and abradant," not only does the unfamiliar adjective *abradant*, with its harsh *d* and *t*, sound more abrasive than the milder, everyday *abrasive*, but its terminal *t* has been bookended with the initial *t* of *tough*, lending symmetry to the adjectives coupled at the sentence's end. And you can take the frumpiest, the ugliest of the so-called vocabulary words—the Latinate monstrosities that students are compelled to memorize in SAT- and GRE-preparation classes—and urge them into a casual setting, where they finally shine anew. Fiona Maazel pulls this off in her sentence "The floor tiles appeared cubed and motile." The choice of the unusual sentence-ending adjective, which in other contexts might risk coming across as thesaurusy and pretentious, most likely resulted from the writer's unwavering alertness to the alphabetics of the noun in the subject slot of her sentence. The upshot of this morphological correspondence between *tiles* and *motile* is that the subject's embrace of its second adjectival complement is much stronger than that which would be achieved by the two words' merely syntactic functions alone. Finally, you can fool around even with prepositions.

Prepositions often attach themselves adverbially to verbs and thus form what are known as phrasal verbs, such as *check out* and *open up* and *see through*, but you are not legally bound to use the orthodox preposition with a verb. Don DeLillo breaks from established usage in the sentences "She was always thinking into tomorrow" and "She moved about the town's sloping streets unnoticed, ... playing through these thoughts...."

Granted, there can be a downside to the kinds of isolative attentions to the sentence I have been advocating. Such a fixation on the individual sentence might threaten the enclosive forces of the larger structure in which the sentences reside. Psychiatrists use the term *weak central coherence* to pinpoint the difficulty of certain autistic persons to get the big picture, to see the forest instead of the trees. A piece of writing consisting ultimately of an aggregation of loner sentences might well strike a reader as stupefyingly discontinuous, too dense to enchant. But the practices I have been trying to discuss can also result in richly elliptical prose whose individual statements converge excitingly in the participating reader's mind. These practices account in part for the bold poetry in some of today's most artistically provocative fiction.

Grateful acknowledgment is made to the editors of the journals in which the entries in this book originally appeared (some in different form and under different titles, and several under the pseudonym Lee Stone):

The Believer: "The Sentence Is a Lonely Place"

Columbia: A Journal of Literature and Art: "Pulls"

New York Tyrant: "Kansas City, Missoula"

NOON: "I Was in Kilter with Him, a Little" and "Partial List of People to Bleach"

The Quarterly: "Home, School, Office," "Six Stories," and "Tic Douloureux"

Sleepingfish: "People Won't Keep" and "You're Welcome"

Soft Targets: "Years of Age"

3:AM: "Loo"

"The Sentence Is a Lonely Place" was delivered as a lecture at Columbia University on September 25, 2008.

Segments of "Heartscald" appeared piecemeal in *Bookslut, elimae, Moistworks, The Quarterly, Salt Hill, Sleepingfish, Soft Targets, The Stranger, 3rd bed,* and *Wag's Review.*

Segments of "Loo" appeared piecemeal in *The Believer, Big Other, The Faster Times, The Fiddleback, New York Tyrant, The Rumpus, Sleepingfish, Soft Targets, The Stranger,* and *Wag's Review.*

With deepest gratitude to Kevin Sampsell, Gordon Lish, Derek White, Anna DeForest, Lisel Virkler, Amy Albracht, and Bryan Coffelt.

CPSIA information can be obtained at www.ICGtesting.com
Printed in the USA
BVOW07s1534230713

326508BV00002B/3/P